ONE WAY TO WHITEFISH

ONE WAY TO
WHITEFISH

Anita Bushell

Douglass Street Books   Brooklyn

Douglass Street Books
Brooklyn, NY

Copyright © Anita Bushell 2024

Designed by Jonathan D. Lippincott

ISBN: 979-8-218-49247-2

This book is dedicated to my family, and my parents, and all those who came before me in the neighborhood known as Yorkville.

ONE WAY TO WHITEFISH

1941

It was cold and icy on Bank Street that day. The February chill permeated everything, including the heavy, wool overcoat Sergei Vasiliev wore, as he carried a brown paper grocery bag and reached into his pocket for his house key.

Letting himself into the vestibule, then the hallway, he held onto the key, again inserting it into the lock of the grey wooden door on the right. Entering his apartment, he brought the bag to the small galley kitchen and placed it on the counter. At that moment, there was a knock at the window.

Sergei walked over and lifted the Venetian blind. Opening the door and going into the vestibule, Sergei let a man, in a thick navy blue wool jacket and Fedora, inside.

"Mr. Frank, hello! Come, step inside, it is so cold today."

"Thank you, Mr. Sergei, just for a moment. I have to get back to the restaurant. I would have sent Johnny, but he is home sick with a cold. We got a call for you from Mrs. Velma. She's asking you to call back."

"Ah, thank you so much, Mr. Frank. I am sorry that Johnny is sick and that you had to come all the way over to tell me this. You are sure I cannot get you a cup of tea, for your trouble?"

"No, thank you very much. Some other time, Mr. Sergei. Well, I'd better be getting back now. Stay warm!"

"Yes, thank you. I will come over in the next fifteen minutes, Mr. Frank." With that, Sergei closed the door and went back into the apartment, where he took the eggs and milk from the grocery bag on the counter and placed them in the small humming white refrigerator.

When he was done, he left the apartment, walking to the right to Greenwich Avenue. Making another right, he made his way to the middle of the block, stepping into Frank's Bar and Grill. Mr. Frank was polishing glasses behind the mirrored bar; Sergei nodded at him and made his way to the back of the restaurant, where he entered a dark wooden telephone booth. He placed a nickel into the circular slot and dialed RE 4-2700.

"Hallo," he said into the black receiver. "Ah, Velma . . . please, you are in the bar. Speak in English. Yes . . . no, I just come home. I go to get groceries at market. Yes, of course . . . is it urgent? You are alright? Come whenever you please . . . I will be home for rest of the afternoon. Goodbye," said Sergei, as he hung up the telephone and left the booth, waving to Mr. Frank as he left the bar.

Back in his apartment, Sergei took off his coat and Fedora, removing an envelope from the breast pocket and placing it in the desk drawer. He then hung the coat in a small closet in the living room and placed the hat on the shelf above the coat. He returned to the kitchen to unpack his groceries. Sardines, dark bread, and a packet of tea all came out of the bag and were placed in the white cabinet above the stove. Sergei then took out a small tin from the cupboard and emptied the tea from the packet into it. Filling the metal kettle with water, Sergei lit a match and held the open flame to the gas, as he turned the stove knob. When contact was made and a blue glow emerged from the front burner, Sergei placed the kettle on top of it, and retreated into the living room.

On the coffee table was a copy of *The New York Times* and the *Novoye Russkoye Slovo*. Sergei sat down on the tan-colored leather couch and pulled a pair of horn-rimmed glasses from his shirt pocket, putting them on as he reached for the Russian newspaper.

Reading for a few minutes about the fire on the S.S. Normandie, an ocean liner that was being converted into a troop ship at Pier 88, he removed his glasses and put down the paper. *What does Velma want,* he thought, *that she is travelling all the way downtown in such weather to see me about?* At that moment, the kettle began to whistle, and Sergei put the paper down on the couch and went into the kitchen to make tea.

The rest of the morning was spent doing chores such as sprinkling sand across the icy sidewalk, and sitting at the desk in the living room, where Sergei paid the bills. He examined the hardware and utility invoices for the building, which he owned, having purchased it from a Russian immigrant friend who had moved with his wife to Montana. He also wrote out the rent receipts for his upstairs tenants—Miss Hammond, on the second floor and Mr. Smith, on the third floor—in a long receipt book. He then entered these amounts in a small black ledger. When he was done, he took the receipt book and ledger, and let himself out of the apartment. Walking to the end of the hallway he stopped at a door under the stairs, which he unlocked with a key that was attached to a chain in his pocket. Switching on an overhead light, he descended the stairs to the basement, where he knelt in front of a steel grey safe, turning the dial left to 17, right to 35, left to 20, and right to 57. After placing the receipt book and ledger in the small drawer, Sergei pulled out a metal lock box and took out a small key from the chain. Inserting the key into the lock, he opened the lid and inspected the gold coins and paper rubles that were nestled in small compartments in the box.

Sergei's parents, Maksim and Natalia, had gone into hiding in the Soviet Union in the fall of 1936, after sending Sergei "on business" for their import/

export operation to Paris. They had entrusted him with their savings, showing him how to hide rubles in the interior lining of his leather suitcase. They had gotten word of their safety to him in New York through a friend but in recent months he had not heard from them. He tried to put all fearful thoughts out of his mind.

He closed and locked the box, replaced it in the safe, and shut the door. When he had turned the dial to make sure the safe was locked again, he climbed the stairs to the first floor, turning out the light behind him.

After a lunch of sardines and cream cheese on dark bread and tea, Sergei swept the apartment with a broom from the narrow kitchen closet, then sat down at the desk again and opened the drawer. Pulling out a silver lighter and pale blue pack of Gauloise cigarettes—a habit picked up in Paris on one of his multiple trips for his family, Sergei's only luxury—he lit one and leaned back in the chair, observing the flat grey day outside the window. *Why does Velma want to come all the way downtown on a day like this?* Sergei wondered. *I hope it is not anything serious.*

When he was finished, he put out the cigarette in the gold-tone ashtray on the desk; he then got up and went over to the couch, lying down and closing his eyes, with his hands resting on his chest. Sleep came easily, as well as dreams, in which a little boy ran through a grand house in the Russian countryside, holding something he had made for his mother.

"Mama, mama!" he called. "Ya sdelal tebe ch-toto!" The boy ran into her arms and handed her a crown of wheat.

"Kak milo!" his mother said, taking the crown from him and giving him a kiss on his head.

At 3:00 p.m. there was a knock at the window. Sergei blinked his eyes several times and slowly sat up before he rose to open the front door.

"Privet, moya dorogoya," he greeted Velma, af-ter he had closed and locked the door, giving her a kiss on each cheek.

"Privet, Sergei," Velma returned the greeting.

Velma was dressed in a navy blue wool overcoat and short black leather boots. She removed a grey patterned scarf that she had been wearing around her head.

"Come, sit," Sergei directed Velma to the sofa. "Chai?"

"Da, spocebo," Velma replied.

Sergei proceeded into the kitchen, where he re-peated the routine of preparing tea, boiling more water, and spooning the loose flakes from the tin into the polished blue teapot on the counter. He then stirred the tea before returning to the living room and sitting back down next to Velma.

"Now, tell me, what is it that you want to dis-cuss?" Sergei asked.

"Sergei, you know Mr. Smolnecki . . . he come to fix things at bar sometimes . . ."

"Yes, I know Mr. Smolnecki," replied Sergei.

"Well," Velma continued, "he come by on

Thursday to fix door to back room and we start talking. He tell to me that his mother is very sick and that she will probably die soon. This make me so sad . . ."

"Yes, I understand . . ." said Sergei.

"But," Velma said, "he tell to me that he no have money to bury her when she die. 'Ach, this is terrible,' I say to him."

Sergei looked at the window; through the blinds he could see large snowflakes gently falling. He then turned back to face Velma.

"I wonder, Sergei," said Velma, "could we help Mr. Smolnecki and lend to him some money?"

Sergei looked at Velma and leaned back on the couch. He took in a deep breath.

"Now we have bar working but we still have money left over in safe," she continued "and what do we do with the rest of money?" Velma asked.

"Well, my dear, there are lots of things we can do with the money I am holding for Mother and Father . . . of course, now that America has entered the war, I don't know if it is the time to lend money. After all, we may need it ourselves, in case we need to leave town."

"Leave town?" Velma asked, with an even more concerned look on her face.

"Yes, well, you know as well as I, that war brings uncertainty; I have no doubt Manhattan will become a target . . ." Sergei looked at Velma, unsure of how these words would affect her.

Velma turned away. She looked around the room.

Everything is so neat and orderly, she thought. *Just like Sergei.*

"Now that we are here," Velma said, "we must believe in President Roosevelt and pray that all will be fine. I cannot think that a little money to Mr. Smolnecki to bury his mother, it prevent us from using the money in other ways, if we need to . . ."

Sergei heard the tea kettle and got up to go into the kitchen. "Moya dorogaya, I will give this some thought," Sergei said as he turned off the kettle and opened the cabinet, producing two cups and saucers.

"You have thoughts for money?" Velma asked, getting up and walking to the kitchen, while Sergei poured the tea into the cups and began spooning apricot preserves from a jar into a small dish.

"Well," Sergei responded, "when you and I came to New York, it was always my thought that we would go to the country, at some time. America is such a big place and there is land to be bought that could be farmed. My dream is that we buy a small place somewhere where we can grow wheat."

"Ach, just like your family . . ." said Velma.

"Yes, just like my family," Sergei answered. "What is wrong with that?"

"No, nothing, there is nothing wrong with this . . . it would be good for the boy . . ." Velma mused.

"Yes, precisely, it would be good for Don. It is well that he helps you in the bar, and that he learns to work, but he should also run around outdoors and breathe in the fresh air. No, my dear, New York, it is no place for a growing boy, if one can avoid it."

Sergei placed the teapot, cups and saucers, and preserves on a tray, which he carried to the living room. "Come," he said to Velma, as they returned to the couch.

"You see, we could have our own dacha, with someone to help us farm . . ." Sergei continued.

"But we can get money back, no?" asked Velma. "We lend money, not give to Mr. Smolnecki. He give to us back."

"One thing," mused Sergei, "if we were to lend money to Smolnecki, we could charge a small interest."

"Interest?" asked Velma.

"Yes, interest . . ." Sergei continued. "When you agree to the amount of money that the person needs, but you charge a little more for the privilege of lending the money. It is a fee."

"Ach, yes, of course," Velma replied.

"This is something I would have to think about because, moya dorogaya, you know what this will lead to . . ." Sergei warned.

"Lead to?" asked Velma.

"Once you lend money to Smolnecki," said Sergei, "then all the neighborhood will know that there is money to be had to bury their dead. You know, we have a little money in the safe, but, after all, I am not a bank."

"Yes, but Sergei, you think about this. My Sasha—your brother—is gone, tossed away like a dead animal in Siberia . . ." Velma looked away.

Sergei pulled a white handkerchief from his pants pocket and handed it to Velma, taking her hands. "We must be strong, moya dorogaya," he said.

"I still cannot believe that this is true. When we hear this news . . ." Velma's voice trailed off. "I think, every day, he will come here and be with us. He will be alive and he will see his son." She paused. "If it were your mother and you have no money to bury her, you want a Sergei in your life to help you, no?"

Sergei took a sip from his teacup. "It is a tragedy that Sasha is gone. I can only imagine that he could not take any more hard labor; he must have said something that they shot him." Sergei took a deep breath. "He was always such an idealistic young man . . ."

Velma dried her eyes and took another sip of her tea.

"However," Sergei said, "We must continue to hope that Mother and Father are safe. He paused. "I shall think about this idea of yours."

They sat together in silence. The sound of teacups clinking on saucers was interrupted by a car outside, honking its horn.

"Wait," Sergei said. "I just remember. There is something I once heard about. In England. There is something—what is it called?" Sergei closed his eyes. "Yes. It is called a 'burial . . . burial . . . society.' That's it. It is called *burial society*. Let me recall how this works . . . I read about it in the paper. Someone dies in the village and the people who are members of the burial society help pay for the funeral. Yes, this is how it works. The members of the burial society have put in money every month. This is how there is enough money to pay for the funeral."

"Ach, I see . . ." said Velma.

"So, you see, we do not lend the money to Smolnecki. We get everyone in the bar to start a burial society. Each person, they put in, let us say, one dollar a month. This is how you start."

Velma continued to drink her tea. The room began to fill with sunlight as the snowflakes settled onto the ground outside.

"You go back to Smolnecki," Sergei continued. "You tell him that you have come up with a way to pay for the funeral. We will start a burial society in the community. Everyone will contribute a certain amount, monthly. I will come up with an initial fee and contribution. For Smolnecki, I will what they call *front* the money for the funeral, and you will begin collecting the dues from the patrons of the bar. Eventually, I will get my money back. But, moya dorogaya, you must be clear with Smolnecki that you are not *giving* him the money, but that the community is starting the burial society. The money he puts back in will pay for the next person's burial.

"Yes," Velma said, finishing her last sip of tea. "This is good. The people, they come together and help Smolnecki and his family. Then this can help other families with proper burial." Velma looked at Sergei. "Yes."

CHAPTER ONE

1957

Don looked around the living room but there was nothing left to see.

His bag was packed, and the apartment was empty. The sun was setting, and the evening light was beginning to come through the Venetian blinds. Don, who was twenty years of age, dark-haired and slender, looked at his watch. He certainly didn't need an hour-and-a-half to get to the Greyhound station, but he also didn't need to sit around the apartment anymore. He had taken care of all the last-minute details. There was nothing left for him to do but leave.

The evening was cool for November, forty degrees, and sandwiched between the Manhattan buildings lining 82nd Street were flaming red stripes crossing the western sky. As Don walked up to Lexington Avenue, he noticed that the colors of the brick houses matched some of the clouds ahead of him. Then his mind turned to food and drink. He had sandwiches and a Thermos full of coffee in his backpack, which would have to be refilled at some point. It was going to be a long ride.

On Lexington, he turned right and walked to 86th Street, where he caught the downtown local train—the number 4—then transferred to the shuttle, at 42nd Street. From Times Square, he made his way to Eighth Avenue, and the Greyhound Bus Terminal, where he approached a ticket window. "Could I have a one-way ticket to Whitefish, please?" he asked the clerk, whose dark hair was braided and pulled back in a bun.

"Whitefish?"

"Oh, sorry, ma'am. I meant Whitefish, Montana," Don replied awkwardly.

"Well, why didn't you say so?" she paused, looking at her master schedule. "The next bus is at 8:30 p.m., with transfers in Chicago, Minneapolis, Billings and Missoula. Total travel time is 66 hours."

"Sixty-six hours," Don repeated. "Geez . . ."

"Yeah, that's gonna be a long one," the ticket agent said. "Hope you got a good book to read." She looked over her eagle-eye glasses at Don. "That'll be $24.50, sonny."

Don reached into the back pocket of his jeans and pulled out a neatly, wadded roll of bills. He pulled off a ten- and a twenty-dollar bill and handed them to the ticket agent.

"Thirty dollars," she said. That'll be five dollars, fifty cents in change," she stated, as she reached into her cash box and pulled out five singles and two quarters. "Here ya go," she said as she started handing Don the bills, individually. "One, two, three, four, five, and fifty cents is your change. You'll find your bay on the departure sign above my window. Safe travels, sonny."

"Thank you, ma'am," Don said, as he placed the change in the cash roll and put it back in his pocket. Don stepped back to look at the destination board. Chicago: 8:30 p.m., Bay 12.

This was Don's first road trip alone. He had never left New York by himself. A bus was certainly not his first choice—he would have preferred a train—but trains were pricey, so Don had no choice but to get to know Greyhound. He was prepared. He had sandwiches and hot, black coffee. He also had a book, Agee's *A Death in the Family,* that he had found in a used bookstore in Yorkville. Hell, for sixty hours, he might even finish it.

Don looked around the station to see where Bay 12 was. When he located it to his right, he walked over and got on line with the other passengers to board the bus. When the driver finally opened the door, he climbed aboard and located a window seat. He loaded his backpack onto the overhead rack and sat down, suddenly feeling bulky and constricted. As he did so the fishing vest he was wearing under his clothing cut into his waist. He was also beginning to sweat. The money, all $12,000 of it, was making him hot.

CHAPTER TWO

1941

"Ma!" Don yelled.

He held the telephone receiver in his hand, from the payphone at the back of the bar, "Mr. Antonio wants to know how many cases this week?" He wished he didn't have to be Velma's secretary.

Don hated the telephone, which helped him develop an aversion to being social. Vendors, supposed friends and the occasionally desperate all called Velma and if Don was working the bar he was forced to answer and sometimes take a message.

"I have to count," Velma would yell from the back room, which served as Velma's office. "You tell to him I call in ten minutes."

"Okay, Ma," Don responded, knowing he would most likely be the one calling Mr. Antonio back with the order.

The back room contained a roll-top desk with a swivel chair and a cot, where friends and patrons of the bar occasionally stayed the night. Velma's rule, though, was that she didn't mind being hospitable, but no one stayed more than one night. "I no operate boarding house," she always said.

The bar, which was located on 84th Street near Second Avenue, was dark and narrow with a floral and geometric patterned tile floor. There was a window with *Velma's* stenciled in gold letters and red-checked half curtains in front of the window seat. Regulars sometimes sat there on a crowded Saturday night. The bar always smelled of smoke. Occasionally, fiery sunlight would overtake dust particles floating across the worn wood. The ceiling was milky beige pressed tin and there were several small opaque light fixtures hanging over the bar that illuminated the ever-present smoke floating up from patron's fingers.

Don started helping Velma in the bar when he was four. Other kids got to "go down," after they got home from school and did their homework, playing together on stoops and sidewalks in front of their buildings. Don had to drop off his books in the apartment around the corner, at 82nd Street and Third Avenue, then go help Velma at the bar. One of his responsibilities was counting out the money with Velma. He would pull down a chair from a table and bring it into the back room. They would sit at the desk, while Velma pulled out her lock box, which was in a small grey safe in the corner, and count the money the bar had made the night before. Sometimes, when the other kids on the block were roller skating or playing hopscotch or stick ball, Don would put down the quarter he was holding and listen to their voices, longing to be outside with them.

"Dontchik," Velma would say, "you no pay attention."

"Okay, Ma," Don would say, and reluctantly get back to counting the money.

On Friday nights, Don and Velma would visit his uncle Sergei, who lived in Greenwich Village. They would walk across 82nd Street to take the bus downtown. As they walked Don noticed the differences in the neighborhood. When they crossed Third Avenue, Don saw that it didn't look like Second Avenue, where there were German and Hungarian food shops and restaurants that extended in both directions. On Third Avenue, there were bars and pawn shops and the two-floor Hayman & Sumner, where Velma often sent Don to buy paper-clips and accounting ledgers.

What was overpowering about Third was the El subway line, occasionally rattling overhead and sending spider-like shadows onto the streets on sunny days. At Lexington, there was the Optimo Cigar store, and the Lexington Candy Shop, where Don occasionally went to grab an egg cream at the fountain with the money he had made running errands. On Park Avenue, there were trees and the streets suddenly seemed much cleaner. Here, people dressed differently and got into yellow Checker taxicabs. They didn't seem as busy or rushed as the folks on Second Avenue.

At Fifth, the bus would proceed through the 70s,

then the 60s, with the grand apartment buildings on the left and Central Park, twinkling with streetlights in between trees, on the right. In the 50s, the park disappeared, and Midtown, with its stores and large churches took its place on both sides of Fifth. Don watched as I. Miller and Tiffany & Co. appeared, then Saks Fifth Avenue, St. Patrick's Cathedral, and the 42nd Street library. He was fascinated by that huge building and wondered whether it was filled with books. One day, he hoped to find out. He imagined himself sitting there surrounded by stacks of books to read.

After 34th Street, the department stores, such as Lord & Taylor and B. Altman, gave way to one- and two-story establishments whose lights were turned off, now that it was after business hours. There were a lot of furniture sellers and Persian rug shops. Compared to the brightly colored windows and streetlamps of Midtown this stretch seemed very dark, and there was something slightly ominous about the neighborhood.

After 23rd Street, there was a narrow diner named S&P Sandwich Shoppe, then at 14th Street, Fifth Avenue became residential again. Velma and Don would get off at 12th Street and pass the beautiful old First Presbyterian Church on the way to Sergei's.

One Friday, on a chilly October evening, Velma stopped Don as they were walking in the middle of 12th Street, between Fifth and Sixth Avenues.

"Ach, where is my head?" she asked.

"What, Ma?"

"I forget to bring cookies!" she exclaimed. "I so busy today I no get them."

"Oh," Don responded. "Maybe we can find a bakery on the way."

"Yes, this is good idea. Come, we go. Maybe there is bakery on Six Avenue."

When they got to the corner of Sixth and 12th Street, Velma and Don looked around. They didn't see a bakery. Velma nudged Don's arm.

"You ask someone where is bakery," she said.

"Okay, Ma," Don replied, looking around. He saw a man in a Fedora hat, glasses, and overcoat walk by.

"Excuse me, mister?" Don asked.

"Yes?" the man replied, stopping to look down at Don and then back up at Velma.

"My mother wants to know, is there a bakery on this street?"

"A bakery . . ." the man repeated as his eyes wandered the avenue, first to the right and then to the left. "Why yes, there is. Juliet Pastry Shop," he said, pointing south. "It's a half block down, between 11th and 12th Streets. They have delicious goodies there."

"Gee, thanks, mister. C'mon Ma," Don said as they turned right.

At Juliet Pastry Shop, there were drawings of Paris on the pale green walls, and it smelled like a vanilla cake was baking in an oven. Velma purchased a pound of assorted cookies, which the older gentleman behind the counter wrapped in green-and-white striped twine that came out of a golden egg that was suspended from the ceiling. Don was fascinated by this process and could not take his eyes off the twine coming out of the egg and how the man deftly worked the twine around a white cardboard box. He then placed the box in a white paper shopping bag that had *Juliet Pastry Shop* scrolled across it in cursive handwriting. The man looked down at Don.

As he handed Velma the bag, he asked Don if he would like a cookie.

"Sure!" Don said, looking up at Velma.

The man smiled, and asked Don which one he would like from the assortment.

There were thumb prints, and black-and-whites, and butter cookies in various shapes. "That one, please," Don said, pointing at a small vanilla cookie that looked like a fan wearing a chocolate skirt.

"Ah, the classic Madeleine. The boy has good taste!" the man said, handing Don the cookie wrapped in a piece of wax paper. Don noticed that it was still warm.

"Dontchik, what do you say?" demanded Velma, nudging him on the shoulder.

"Thank you," Don said, mechanically.

"You're welcome" the man said. "And Madame . . . for you? Could I give you one, as well? These are fresh out of the oven!"

"For me?" Velma asked. "Yes," she said. "Thank you," and she took the cookie from the gentleman's hand. Don looked up at Velma. She was smiling. Velma never smiled.

Velma handed Don the shopping bag and they were about to exit the store when Velma exclaimed. "Ach, look, it rains."

Don looked out the door. People were walking with umbrellas. "We will get wet," Velma said. Looking around the bakery she came up with an idea. "Come, we sit for a moment until the rain, it stops." Then, to the man behind the counter, Velma asked, "Is it okay, we sit for few minutes until rain stops? We forget umbrellas."

"Yes, of course, sit! We close in thirty minutes. You have plenty of time!" the man said. "Perhaps I bring you a cup of hot tea? Nothing like a cup of tea on a night like this."

"Tea, yes, thank you," Velma responded. "Tea is what we need, right Dontchik?"

Don looked at Velma. He was surprised by this turn of events. They never went out to eat together and certainly not for treats like this. They settled down at a table when the gentleman came over. He had a small white plate of extra Madeleines and a little metal pot of boiling water, as well as two cups with tea bags and saucers.

"There we are," he said. "Just what one needs on a night like this—a cup of hot tea and a Madeleine! I brought you some extra because it's the end of the day. On the house!" he said, winking at Velma.

"Wow!" Don smiled, as he grabbed another cookie from the plate.

"Thank you very much," Velma said, looking up at the man. "You very kind."

"A pleasure, Madame," the man responded, smiling at Velma, and walking away. Don looked at the man as he walked back to the counter, then took another bite.

Velma and Don quietly sipped their tea and munched on their Madeleines. Don wondered why they didn't get a chance to do things like this more often.

"Ma?" Don asked, while he ran his fingers along the lines of his treat.

"Yes, Dontchik?" Velma replied.

"Why does Uncle Sergei live so far away from our house?" Don asked.

"Well, Dontchik, you see, we have friend—you know, Ivan—who comes to bar on Saturday night."

"Sure, I know who Ivan is," said Don.

"Well," Velma continued, "Ivan, he bought buildings in Manhattan when he come here."

"Uh huh . . ." Don replied.

"So, you see," Velma continued, "Ivan own building on Bank Street where Sergei live and he sell to Sergei, when he leave New York."

"Oh, I get it," Don answered. "Why did he leave New York?"

"Ach, Dontchik," Velma exclaimed, "always so many questions. Ivan and his wife, Nina—you re-member her?—they move far away, to place called Montana, to be near her family there."

"Montana," repeated Don. "That's out West, isn't it?"

"Yes, Dontchik. It is in West," Velma replied.

After a few minutes, she turned to look out the window. The rain had stopped. "Come, we go," Velma said, as she reached into her pocketbook for her change purse to pay the gentleman at the counter.

"Let's see," the man said " . . . that'll be two teas, and it's the end of the day, so the Madelines are on the house. Twenty cents for the two teas, please."

"Twenty cents," Velma repeated, and snapped open her black leather change purse, taking out four dimes. "Here is forty cents. Please to keep change," Velma said, handing the man the money.

"Thank you very much, Madame," the man said. "Have a good evening."

"Goodbye," Velma said, "and thank you very much."

"Any time, Madame, any time," the man said, smiling again at Velma.

Don and Velma exited into the inky night, with its sleek, wet pavements, and glistening cars making a swooshing sound with their tires. They walked west on 12th Street until they got to Seventh Avenue South, where they crossed over to Bank Street.

Several doors in on Bank, there was a narrow building, three stories high. Velma rang the first bell, and after a minute Sergei emerged to let them in. Inside the vestibule, then hallway, they entered the railroad apartment to the right that extended to the back of the building. The front was the living room, the back was the bedroom and, sandwiched in the middle, there was a small galley kitchen and bathroom on the side.

Sergei always greeted Don by tousling his hair. "Well, Don, how is my boy?" he would always ask. Sergei was a man in his late forties, with light-colored hair that was combed back. He wore navy blue flannel pants and a white shirt. He always carried his horn-rimmed reading glasses in his shirt pocket.

"Dobrey vecher," Sergei said, as he embraced Velma, giving her a kiss on each cheek. "Come. Let me take your coat." He took Velma's coat and placed it on the bed in the back room. Don followed them and left his coat, as well, taking his time to poke around Sergei's apartment, one of Don's favorite pastimes.

Don and Velma went into the kitchen with Sergei, who took the shopping bag from Don and started unpacking the cookies onto a serving plate. At this point, Velma and Sergei started speaking Russian.

This was always Don's cue to go into the living room where there was a camel-colored leather sofa and armchair in the corner. There was a circular coffee table in front of the sofa. A bookshelf along the wall had an English dictionary, a one-volume encyclopedia, and several novels in Russian by Vladimir Nabokov. White Venetian blinds covered the windows.

A desk by the window had a long, gooseneck lamp and a stack of the daily newspapers on it, including *The New York Times*, the *New York Herald Tribune* and *Novoe Ruskoe Slovo*. One of the things Don loved about Sergei's apartment was that there were so many ways for him to occupy himself. Most of all, he liked to sit at the desk and scribble on the steno writing pad with one of the pencils he found in the leather pencil cup; he also loved to test out the fountain pen on the dark green blotter. Sergei didn't mind, and often left out scrap writing paper, such as old commercial mail he no longer needed, for Don to draw on.

Often, Don and Velma were the first of several guests to arrive. Everyone brought beer and sandwiches, Wise potato chips and cookies for dessert. The best part was that Don got to drink Coca-Cola, a treat Velma only allowed at these Friday night gatherings and other special occasions.

Early in the evening, as the other guests started to wander in, Don was the center of attention, since he was the only child there. "How is school?" a German woman, with short, sand-colored hair and blue eyes named Susanna asked. "What did you learn today?" came from Johann, a stocky man with combed-back blond hair and rosy skin. As the evening wore on, though, Don's presence receded into the background and the adult conversation, beer and cigarettes took over. In between his wanderings through the paper clip jar at Sergei's desk—where he liked to link a set together to make a chain—and the potato chip bowl—which he periodically visited to fill a wax paper beverage cup with chips—Don heard discussions regarding how things were progressing in Europe and what a man named Hitler was up to. Don seemed to hear this name more and more often lately.

More often than not, Don—after too much Coca Cola and potato chips that Velma, uncharacteristically, did not notice—would fall asleep sitting at Sergei's desk, lifting his heavy head only when Velma would wake him, around 10:30 p.m. "Come, we go home. Mr. Smolnecki, he drive us."

Stumbling, Don would make his way with Velma into the cool night air to Mr. Smolnecki's parked yellow taxicab, which he drove for a living. Friday evening was his night off. Don, half asleep, sandwiched between Velma and Mr. Smolnecki, would stare at the red taillights of the cars ahead of them. As they made their way up Sixth Avenue, cutting across 57th Street, then uptown on Third Avenue to 82nd Street, Don kept thinking that the red taillights reminded him of Christmas tree balls. Then he would fall back asleep on Velma's lap.

Climbing up the stairs of the tenement, Don felt as if his legs were made of mush. He barely made it to the second floor, where he collapsed, while Velma undressed him, in his little bedroom at the back of the apartment.

CHAPTER THREE

1957

Don woke up with a start, finding a bag of cosmetics on his lap.

"Oh my Lord, I am so sorry. The bus jolted and I lost my case," a female voice said.

Don looked up and saw a young woman kneeling over him and picking up the toothbrush, toothpaste and comb that had spilled out. He stared at the woman while rubbing his eyes.

Don had been dreaming about being at home and a cigar box he kept on the top shelf in his closet. He had found it one Saturday afternoon in the trash outside the Optimo store on Lexington Avenue. It was his secret box. To get to it he had to climb on top of his desk chair, which he would pull over to the closet. Sometimes, if he had too many things stashed on the top shelf the box would come tumbling down, the contents crashing on his head.

The woman was dark haired and probably in her late twenties. He looked out of the window but could not tell what station they had just pulled out of. The stiffness in his back and the jabbing in his sides reminded him that he was going to have to get out and walk around sometime soon.

"Is this seat taken?" the woman nervously asked. Don noticed she was shaking. She reached over to hold on to the overhead rack as the bus began to lurch again. Not sure if he was awake or dreaming, Don tried to find the words to respond.

"No, uh, no it's not," Don stammered, wondering when he would get the chance to fill up his Thermos with some strong hot coffee.

"Thank you," the young woman said, placing her small cream-colored valise in the overhead rack and almost collapsing into the seat next to Don. He slightly turned his head towards her direction and noticed that she was wearing a brown wool day dress and matching heels. Her coat, which she wore around her shoulders, was a soft, black cashmere. She was lovely but looked tired and worn, as if she had not slept in some time.

"Um, miss, could you tell me where we are?" Don asked her.

"Oh, yes, we just pulled out of Cleveland," the woman responded, giving Don a faint smile. She leaned back against the seat and closed her eyes. It was just at this moment that Don suddenly realized he needed to use the bathroom at the back of the bus. He didn't want to wake the young woman up, though, if she was going to fall asleep.

"Excuse me," Don said, as he attempted to get up and awkwardly step over her. The young woman opened her eyes.

"Oh, I'm sorry, am I in your way?"

"I think I can make it. Sorry to bother you, miss," Don said, apologetically.

When he returned from the bathroom, the young woman had indeed fallen asleep. Don noticed that a tear had run down the right side of her face. Not knowing what to do, he stood there, holding the side of the overhead rack. He looked around. Maybe there was an empty seat he could take while the young woman slept. He did not want to wake her, especially since she had been crying.

Don saw that there was a seat available across the aisle and one row back, next to an older man in a dark blue suit and tie by the window, asleep, with a newspaper open on his lap. Don reached into the overhead compartment to take his Thermos and sandwich out of his backpack, then slid into the seat, hoping that no one would come to claim it. From here, he could observe the woman and would be able to see when she woke up.

As he poured what was left of the now tepid black coffee into the metallic green Thermos cup and unwrapped his cheese and salami sandwich he looked at the clouds hanging over the harvested cornfields passing by. Everything was flat and the sky seemed washed out. Don took a bite of his sandwich, following it with a swig of coffee and felt sleepy again. He wrapped up his sandwich, finished his coffee and replaced the cap, getting up to put everything back in his backpack. After he did so, he sat back down in the seat and closed his eyes, feeling the joints in the road, which made a rhythmic sound as the bus passed over them, one after another, one after another.

The sound was like a drum beaten in time. The drummer, who was unseen, maneuvered his sticks on Don's head, ba-rum, ba-rum, as he made his way down the tracks, struggling to not fall through the slats. He kept following the train, but it was always ahead of him, and Don could never catch up. On the last car was a window and in it a young woman, with soft, dark hair. She was standing and waving at Don. As the train slowed down and pulled into the next station, Don thought he could finally catch up. Just as he made it to the last car, he reached out to climb on board, and the train started pulling away, slowly it seemed, but rapidly enough that he could never catch up. Don kept running down the tracks, but the train kept moving away in front of him.

"Are you okay, son?" someone asked, just as Don tried to grab on to the railing of the last train car. He hit his head on the seat in front of him and found himself staring into the face of the man in the dark blue suit.

Don rubbed his head. "Oh, I'm sorry, I must have fallen asleep," he said to the man. "I hope I didn't disturb you."

"No trouble at all," the man said. "You didn't hit your head too hard, did you?" the man asked.

"No, I think I'm fine, thank you," Don said.

"Glad to hear it," the man said, going back to his newspaper.

"Excuse me," Don said as he got up to go back to his seat. He looked down and noticed that the woman was still asleep.

CHAPTER FOUR

1944

When Don was seven, he began washing and polishing the glasses and accepting deliveries of beer. The bar mostly served Pabst Blue Ribbon, Rheingold and Schlitz. For the regulars who preferred something harder there was also Schnapps, rye and vodka.

Sometimes, if Velma could spare him, the regulars gave Don Saturday-morning delivery jobs of their own. He liked these jobs—they gave him some pocket change. Velma never paid him. There was Mr. Joe, who owned Schein Drug, who would call Don when his regular boy was out sick. Don would run over and bring a prescription to an elderly person or someone too ill to make it out the door. Don liked running deliveries for Mr. Joe. He often gave him a quarter: "Here, go over and get yourself something at Kramer's." Don loved stepping into the bakery, with its steamy windows and overpowering scent of apples and butter. Mrs. Prohuszka, from Magyar Hungarian Grocery, would also call him when she was short staffed. He would walk into the shop, with its sawdust-covered floor, and smell of paprika and sausage. Mrs. Prohuszka would hand Don grocery items to bag in brown paper sacks that he would deliver down the street.

One Saturday in May, Velma pushed open his bedroom door, without knocking. Velma never knocked.

"Dontchik, you come!" She nudged him on his shoulder and pulled the bed covers back. Then she left the room.

Don popped open his eyes several times, staring at the crack in the ceiling, his old friend resembling a tree branch that greeted him daily. Turning over, he curled up close to the wall, and pulled the covers back over him, knowing he only had a minute or so before the inevitable return of Velma. He must have drifted off because a few minutes later, he heard, "Dontchik, get up! Please to get dressed." She was standing over Don and pulling down the covers once more.

Don sat up on the edge of the bed and rubbed his eyes. He looked up at Velma. "Ma, what day is it? Isn't today Saturday?" he asked, wondering why she was waking him up, since it wasn't a school day. He tried to lie back down in the bed. Velma, as usual, intervened.

"You dress. We go." Velma said, opening his wooden bureau drawer to take out a white undershirt, a flannel button-down to go over it, and pants for Don to dress in.

"Go where?" Don asked, sitting up again and slowly swinging his feet over the side of the bed. He knew he had already lost the battle he was waging to stay in bed, the way he always did on Saturday mornings, when all he wanted was to sleep late.

"We go to special place," Velma said, leaving the clothing she had pulled out of the drawer laid out on Don's bed, then returning to the kitchen to pour hot tea and milk into an ivory-colored mug for him.

"What special place?" Don asked. "Where is it? Where are we going?"

"You no ask so many questions, Dontchik. It is surprise. Now, you drink your tea" Velma said, handing him the mug, "and I make you breakfast. Then we go!"

"Okay, Ma," Don responded reluctantly, standing up to pick up the clothing Velma had laid out and get dressed. As he pulled on the undershirt and red and navy blue flannel button-down that Velma had laid out on the bed, Don was all wonderment. *We never do anything unplanned. Where could Ma possibly want to go?* There were so many possibilities. *Shopping for new clothing?* Velma wouldn't have held back on her mission. She would just tell him what they were doing. *Going out to eat?* That was a rare occurrence. Velma always cooked and sometimes they ate out with Sergei, but never first thing in the morning. Besides, she was making his breakfast, so that couldn't be it. Maybe one of Velma's friends had opened a new store in the neighborhood and they were going to see it. That could be it.

As Don ate his fried egg and toast at the kitchen table, Velma looked out the window onto Third Avenue. "Dontchik, it looks like rain soon," she said. "Come, you finish and we go, before the rain, it comes. Please to take dishes to sink."

"Okay, Ma," Don said, taking his last sip of tea. He placed his dishes in the white enamel sink in the kitchen and walked to the coat hook on the wall by the front door to get his cap and wool jacket down.

Don and Velma went down the steps of the tenement and turned east on 82nd Street. It was chilly for May and the sky was flat and grey. Don noticed that Velma was carrying a brown paper shopping bag in her hand.

"What's in the bag, Ma?" Don asked.

"You see when we get there," said Velma.

"Get where? Where are we going?" Don asked.

"Ach, my Dontchik, so many questions!" Velma exclaimed, as they continued down 82nd Street. Walking on the street like this, Don realized he and Velma rarely went places together. She was always at the bar, and he ran errands for her on his own. Except when they were at Sergei's, it wasn't very often that they were in the same place at the same time. He wondered why it was like this. Did other kids go places with their parents?

They proceeded, walking hand in hand, as a breeze danced around their faces. As Don wondered where they were headed, he noticed how long the blocks were between Second, First, and York Avenues. At the corner of East End Avenue, Velma said,

"Come, we go left here." Because they were closer to the East River the wind whipped up into their faces.

Suddenly Don noticed something on the sidewalk. "See a penny, pick it up, and all day you'll have good luck!" he exclaimed, picking up a shiny, steel penny off the ground. He held it in his hand and examined it.

"What you find?" asked Velma.

"Look, Ma, a penny!" cried Don.

"A penny! Goodness, what we do with it?" Velma asked.

"Hmmm . . ." Don mused. "I know! Let's make a wish!"

"A wish . . . this is good idea," Velma proclaimed.

Don closed his eyes. "I wish we had a house in the country. With horses and chickens and a river that I could go swimming in!" Don opened his eyes, looking at some trash blowing by him and the soot-colored tenements surrounding them. He turned to Velma. "What do you wish for, Ma?" Velma looked up at the sky.

"Me? Ach . . . what do I wish for . . ." Velma repeated. "I . . . wish . . . for . . ." she closed her eyes. "A day off! Yes . . . this is what I wish . . . a day off."

"A day off?!" Don asked. "That's what you wish for? You could have that anytime you want!" *Adults say the funniest things,* Don thought.

"Yes, you think this, because you are child. Children, they don't know adult world and what adults do. Children live in child's world. I know . . . I was once child, too!" Velma explained as they continued walking north on East End Avenue.

Don never pictured Velma as a child. She was always Velma, with her light blond hair that was beginning to show a little gray at the temples, always tied back with a dark-colored ribbon, and her pale blue eyes. "Ma, what was it like when you were little?" Don asked. He had never asked her this before.

"Dontchik, see, we here," Velma said as Don looked up and saw they were at the entrance to Carl Schurz Park.

"Ma, we're at the park. This is where we're going?" Don was confused.

"Yes, Dontchik, come, you see," Velma said, as they proceeded through the entrance and walked down the path towards the river, where it seemed even windier than outside the park. Don looked around and saw parents and children and people walking dogs.

In the distance Don heard the sound of a tugboat. As they neared the river they turned left and walked along the water on the path, which was made up of hexagonal paving stones. Don loved looking at these shapes as they walked, watching as one shape ended and another immediately began. He started counting them as they went along.

"Look, we here," said Velma, stopping in front of a path that veered off to the left, away from the river. On both sides of the path were vegetables, growing in clusters and on wooden sticks that had been dug into the ground. There were cabbages sprouting from the soil and tomatoes climbing up to the sky. There were even stalks of corn, growing in a miniature-size patch on the other side of the path, behind a sign that read, *Welcome to the Yorkville Victory Garden,* and a dispenser that held pamphlets called *Your Guide to Growing.* Velma led Don to the sign, where she took out one of the pamphlets.

"Wow," Don exclaimed, looking around. "What is this, Ma?"

"This is garden, Dontchik, and we can even grow here, too!" said Velma.

"We can?" Don asked. "You mean, you and I can plant things here? In the park?"

"Yes, this is why I bring tools," said Velma, opening her brown paper bag from which emerged a small shovel, a large fork-like implement, and a packet of seeds in a brightly colored envelope.

"What are those?" asked Don, pointing to the seed packet.

"These," Velma said, holding it up, "are beet seeds. And look," she proclaimed as she pointed to something growing in the ground, "my spinach, it comes up!"

"They are?" Don exclaimed, as he kneeled down to look with Velma. "You planted these?" Don wondered when this could have taken place.

"Yes! They come up nicely, no?" Velma asked, fingering some of her seedlings.

"Wow . . ." Don said, looking around. He walked from plant to plant. "What are these, Ma?"

"Dontchik, look you see," Velma said, pointing down at something in the ground, "there is little sign that tell you what it is growing." Don walked back to where Velma was standing and knelt down in front of some vegetables that were beginning to sprout up from the ground.

"Oh! I see," said Don, who knew how to read and was examining the hand-printed signs. "This one says leeeeks." Don walked a little further. "And this one says let-tuce. And here is one that says on-ions," Don read.

"Dontchik, you read good!" exclaimed Velma.

"Are you going to plant beets today, Ma?" Don asked.

"Yes, and you help me, please," said Velma. "Here, I open seeds and you hold in your hand," she said, ripping the top of the seed packet and pinching it from side to side in order to see what was inside. "Give me your hand, Dontchik."

Don held out his right hand and Velma poured a few of the seeds into it. "Gee, these are funny looking seeds, Ma," Don said, as he examined the curly brown things that resembled tiny brown flow-ers. Don played with them for a few seconds before Velma said, "Dontchik, here . . . please to put into the ground." Velma had taken her large fork and run it across the soil, creating three parallel lines that were about an inch apart.

"You take seeds," Velma said, pointing at Don's open hand, "and you place in here." She took sev-eral seeds from the packet, placed them between her fingers, and inserted them into one of the rows. Don followed suit and tried to place the seeds in the row, but he had too many in his hand.

"Here," Velma said, "I show you," and she helped him transfer the seeds from his right hand to his left. Then he could use his right hand to place the seeds in the row, one by one.

When all of the seeds in the packet were inserted in the rows, Velma said, "Now we cover up the seeds and make soil even." She took her small shovel and started smoothing over the soil until you couldn't see any of the seeds and all the rows had disappeared.

"Yes," Velma said, surveying her work, "now we done for day. We go home." She started putting away the gardening tools in the brown paper bag. As Don put in the last tool, he had a thought. "Ma, we have a back yard, outside. We could plant seeds there!"

"What back yard you talk about, Dontchik?" asked Velma, as they walked back to the 84th Street exit, along the river.

"You know, Ma. Out back, behind the bar!" said Don, excitedly.

"Behind bar? Those just weeds, Dontchik. Nothing grow there," said Velma.

"But we could try, couldn't we?" Don continued. "You and I could plant seeds behind the bar!"

Velma was silent, thinking about this new idea for a moment. "Well, it dark back there and not too much sun," she mused. "But maybe . . ."

"Could we try, Ma? Could we?" asked Don, as he stopped in front of her while they walked.

"Well . . . yes . . . I think we try, Dontchik," Velma replied. "You good boy, Dontchik. You good boy," she said as she took his hand, and they crossed East End Avenue to go back home.

CHAPTER FIVE

1957

Don was sorry Chicago came so soon. After the young woman had woken up, Don resumed his seat next to her and gave her time to get herself together. They began a conversation and ended up speaking until she got off the bus in Chicago, hours later.

"Oh, my, what a mess I am," the young woman said as she looked over to see Don sitting next to her again. She went to work, combing her hair and applying a fresh coat of pale pink lipstick.

"You're no mess at all," Don said.

"Well, thank you. That's very kind of you," she said, looking at him. "I'm Ruth." She gave him her hand.

"My name's Don," he responded, shaking her hand, which felt soft and warm in his.

"I've had a very rough time the past few weeks," she said.

"Oh. I'm so sorry," Don said, surprised at this admission. He didn't know whether he should ask why.

"My mother just passed away suddenly," Ruth continued, "and I barely got to see her before she died." She reached back into her purse to produce a white linen handkerchief, which she used to dab at her right, then her left eye.

"Oh my, how awful." Don said. "That must have been very hard." Don had never spoken to someone close to his age who had lost their mother. He couldn't imagine what it would be like if Velma died. He had never really thought about it.

"Yes, well, the hardest part was I had just started a job as a dress model in Chicago, and I was going to help pay some of my mother's bills. At first, I didn't want to go, but she insisted. Of course, we didn't really know how she sick she was. Perhaps she hadn't told us . . ." Ruth continued to dab at her eyes as her voice trailed off.

"My girlfriend, Caroline, got me the job," she then continued. "It was a great opportunity, and I was excited to try life in the big city. Then my mother fell ill. She collapsed one day at work. She was a secretary at an insurance firm in Cleveland, and they found her on the bathroom floor. Maybe that was why she had been acting so strange lately." Her voice dropped off again as she looked away, out the bus window.

"Strange?" Don asked.

"Yes, her behavior . . . before I left, she had become so moody, and sometimes downright unpleasant to be around. She had never been like that, though. She was always solid, the rock of our family. Hardworking and firm, but she could also be light and fun, as well. My father died when my sister and I were small, and my mother not only raised us but worked at the insurance company, as well, to make sure we had everything we needed. She didn't spoil us, though. She was very much against spoiling children."

"I see," said Don. He had heard the word spoiled before, but never fully grasped what it meant in reference to children.

"Then, one Saturday," Ruth continued, "I had just gotten a letter from my friend, Caroline, about this job opening and I was planning my trip to meet her in Chicago. My mother was never a big drinker, yet I found her at the kitchen table, staring out the window, with a bottle of gin. It was early in the afternoon; I remember thinking, 'Mother never drinks before 5:30, and she rarely drinks anything other than wine or sherry.'"

"Ah," Don said.

"'Mother, is there something wrong?'" I asked.

"'This gin and tonic is so refreshing'" she said. "'Can I make you one?'"

Ruth turned to Don. "I'm really not much of a drinker, so I said no. Then my mother came right out with it: 'I'm not well, Ruth.'"

"'Mother, what do you mean?'" I asked.

"'I've not been myself lately, as you may have noticed, and I finally called the doctor. He sent me to a specialist for x-rays to be taken and it turns out I have a tumor. In my brain.'"

"I didn't know what to say." Ruth continued. "I

suddenly felt weak and had to sit down. It was as if I was watching someone else tell this story about their family. I wasn't in my house, and it wasn't my mother who was telling me this."

"I can only imagine," Don said. "That must have been horrible."

"The thing is—I immediately assumed my mother was going to die. What a terrible thing. I didn't know—maybe her prognosis was going to be a good one. I didn't even give her a chance to tell me. I had already given her up for gone. I suppose I panicked because I couldn't imagine living without her. She had been so strong, taking care of my sister and myself all throughout our childhood, and I couldn't even begin to think about life without her."

"Yes, of course," Don responded, looking out at the white fences and the grazing horses beyond them, as the road whipped by. Don and Velma had never been close like this. Velma loved Don. There was no question about that. They had a different relationship, though, than the one Ruth was describing with her mother.

They continued to talk about Ruth's plans once she got back to Chicago, and how she liked to spend her time, when she wasn't modeling dresses, which included going to museums, reading, and sewing. "One day, I'd love to design and sew dresses of my own," she proclaimed.

"Folks, we'll be pulling into the Chicago terminal in five minutes," the driver announced. "Chicago—five minutes."

"Well, it was very nice talking to you," Ruth rose to get her valise from the overhead compartment.

"Please, let me get that for you," Don insisted. They were both about to get off the bus, Don to make a transfer and Ruth for her final destination. It was that awkward moment, however, when everyone is waiting to get off the bus, and no one is moving. They both looked at each other. Neither seemed to know what to say.

"Well," Ruth said, finally, "if you're ever in Chicago, please look me up at Marshall Field's. I'm Ruth Morgan. Goodbye," she said, as she reached out her hand to Don. Passengers were finally picking up their luggage and exiting the bus.

He held out his hand awkwardly. "Goodbye, Ruth. It was awfully nice talking to you. I wish you the best of luck."

"That's very sweet of you, Don. And to you, as well. Goodbye," she said as Don watched her walk down the sidewalk with her valise in one hand and her purse in the other.

As he made his way to his next bus, Don thought how sorry he was to see Ruth go. He had enjoyed having someone to talk to, and Ruth had made a very nice travelling companion. Now, Don had many quiet hours ahead of him with only *A Death In the Family* to keep him company.

CHAPTER SIX

1947

Kah-TUM, Kah-TUM, Kah-TUM, Kah-TUM, Kah-TUM, Kah-TUM, Kah-TUM, Kah-TUM. Don, ten-years-old, stared at the ceiling while he blew a pink bubble. When he wasn't looking up, he would play with his Double Bubble gum wrapper, folding over the corners to make it into different shapes. Late Saturdays, when Don was on his own, he could while away the afternoon, lying in bed and listening to the Third Avenue El, as it rattled by the building. Sometimes he would sit by the window and wonder where all the people he could see on the subway—men in hats, women wearing lipstick—were going.

Saturdays were Don's favorite day. He had two things he had to accomplish after breakfast, then the day was his. First, he had to do all his home-work. If he hadn't needed to help Velma at the bar on Friday nights, he would do it all then, so he could have the whole weekend to himself.

Then, he had to tend the garden he and Velma had planted at the back of the bar. It had turned out to be much more work than either of them had anticipated.

"This soil—terrible!" Velma proclaimed when they first went out the back door behind the bar. "We will have to bring new soil."

"What are youse, nuts?!" Mrs. Schwartz yelled out her second-floor window one morning. "Youse can't grow anything out there! It's a dump!"

"Yes, is dump. But we try, anyway," Velma responded, looking up at her.

Velma appealed to Sergei, who thought it was more work than she needed but understood that it was Don's idea, and that it would be wonderful for him to learn how to garden. Fresh soil, mulch, as well as seeds, were purchased and Don and Velma went to work one early fall day when it was still warm enough to be outside without having to put on heavy clothing.

First, they raked the leaves that had fallen. Then the old soil was sifted and bits of broken glass and assorted debris that had accumulated over time were pulled out. Next, Don and Velma layered the new soil and planted some daffodil and tulip bulbs, which would bloom the following spring. Finally, beet, turnip, and spinach seeds were distributed, and the mulch was sprinkled on top.

Don loved going out every afternoon he was at the bar to see how things were progressing. If too much time passed without rain, he would fill a large aluminum watering can and go to work hydrating the garden.

One day the following spring, Don came running from the garden into the bar.

"Ma!" he yelled. "Guess what?!"

"Dontchik, what is it?" Velma asked, as she came to the back door, wiping her hands with a dishtowel.

"Look!" Don said, pointing to the garden.

"Ach! Look at this!" Velma proclaimed on seeing the bright yellow daffodils that were starting to come up along the chain link fence.

"And here, look here, Ma!" Don grabbed Velma's hand and led her to the other side of the yard, where the beet, turnip, and spinach seedlings were starting to sprout above the ground. "We did it!"

"Yes, my Dontchik, we did this. You had idea, remember?"

Eventually, the beets, turnips, and spinach all grew large enough to be harvested and eaten.

"I can't believe youse grew anything out here!" Mrs. Schwartz yelled out her window when she saw what they had produced.

"I know, right?!" Don called back to her.

After garden and homework duty, Don was usually released by lunchtime, when he would wander over to Sammy's News and Candy shop on York and 83rd. He would carry change in his pocket from the errands he had done around the neighborhood and stock up on lemon sticks, Mary Janes, Double Bubble, and *Archie* comics for the afternoon. As he walked back home along 82nd Street he would shove two pieces of gum in his mouth while reading about the antics of Archie, Betty, Veronica, and Jughead.

Archie didn't like homework. Don didn't understand this, as he was a good student and rarely got in trouble at school.

There was, however, the schoolyard incident. It took place after lunch on a grey November afternoon. While he was playing tag with one of the boys, Don overheard some kids in the background. Although they didn't call out to him, it seemed like they were talking about him, pointing their fingers, and laughing.

Don stopped running and walked over to them. "Hey! What're you looking at?"

"Nothing," the bigger boy, Tomek, laughed, punching one of the smaller boys, Fred, in the ribs. "Only, it's like this," he said, coming up close to Don and jabbing his index finger into Don's sternum. "Since you're so rich—Don Bon—why don't you share some of your money with your pals at school, huh?"

"Rich?" Don cried out. He was incredulous. "What're you talking about? I ain't rich! Where'd you get a cockamamie idea like that?" Don felt like he was getting hot, even though it was cold out. He wanted to take off his coat and throw it on the ground.

"Ah, my old man says your mother makes the money out back of the bar," Tomek said. "So, I says, why can't I have some, too, huh?" Tomek advanced towards Don, with Fred and the other boy, Joseph, in tow. Some of the other children in the schoolyard were starting to gather around them.

Don stood his ground.

"Listen," he said, getting more and more annoyed. "I don't know what you're talking about and I ain't rich!" Don yelled. He could feel warmth creeping under his skin. Suddenly he was thirsty. Just then, the school bell rang, and Don simply turned around and walked away from the boys through the heavy wooden door to the hallway. "Okay, Don Bon, the rich boy, Don Bon, the rich boy," he could hear them chanting as he opened the door and went back inside.

On the way home from school, Don couldn't stop thinking about Tomek and the schoolyard boys. What were they talking about? And why did they think his mother "made money?" How would she "make" money? She owned a bar. No one at the bar had money. They were all working people. They didn't have any money. They all had jobs, even some of the women, who had gone to work when the men were serving in the war. They spent whatever they had left after paying the bills, which Don heard a lot about, at the bar. Whatever they had left over amounted to change. Not large bills, like the boys at school made it sound.

After reading the comics, Don often dragged his desk chair over to the closet and climbed up to get his Optimo cigar box off the high shelf. Sitting on the bed he would open the box, pulling out all its contents and laying it on the bed.

There were metal horses of varying sizes, match-book covers Don had found from various bars and restaurants, some pennies, nickels dimes, and some keys. There was also a ticket stub from *National Velvet*, which Don had seen at the 86th Street Grande with Velma and Sergei.

Don liked to arrange the horses according to size. Sometimes they would face each other, nuzzling, and often he would have them run across the vast expanse of calico quilt on the cast iron bed. Occasionally, Don would get up and go to his small, roll top desk where there was a Fair Play Composition book tucked away in one of the compartments at the back. He would dig around in one of the little drawers to find a lead pencil and begin to draw the horses and a background for them, making mountains and trees, grasses and other small animals. He always tried to draw a cowboy, but he wasn't very good at human figures. Every time he tried, he found they looked lopsided, or their torsos were too long. Don often wondered what it would be like to take a drawing class where he could learn how to draw people the right way.

He wanted to draw the sun, but he felt funny about making one out of grey, lead pencil. The sun should be yellow. He would simply have to wait until he got a set of Eagle Prismacolor pencils, like the kind he saw the last time he was at Hayman & Sumner. He was saving up for one of these sets from the odd jobs he was doing around the neighborhood.

What he really wanted, though, was a fountain

pen, the kind that Sergei had on his desk. Most of the time Sergei carried this pen in his shirt pocket but would often leave it on the desk when Don visited on Friday evenings. There was something so satisfying about the smoothness of the ink flowing on the paper, its dark blue like the color of the sea. He liked to draw in pencil, but he yearned to see his drawings in color. Maybe even fountain pen and colored pencil? He would draw the mountains and sky in ink. If there was water, he would definitely use ink for that, as well. Everything else would be in color. Green for trees and plants, reds and pinks for flowers and brown for earth and mountains.

Don first discovered drawing at Sergei's. It began with scribbling, out of boredom, with lead pencils and ball point pens as he sat at Sergei's desk while the adults did their eating, drinking and talking. Eventually, the scribbling turned into drawing animals and objects. Don had tried to draw some of the characters from the Archie comic strip, but they never came out right.

Sometimes Don would find pencils on the street. They would often be small and stubby, having been used a lot by their owners. They would usually have a little or no eraser, but as long as there was lead left Don would pick up the pencil, bring it home and restore it back to life, sitting on the side of his bed and sharpening the pencil with the small, red Swiss Army knife that Sergei had given him for his eighth birthday. Once, when Don was walking home from one of his odd jobs, he found a canvas pencil case on the street filled with Eagle *Mirado* pencils of varying sizes, almost all with their erasers intact. Don felt like he had found a ten-dollar bill.

Often, when the weather was nice, Don would take part of his Saturday afternoon and walk over to Central Park. Even though it was only fifteen minutes away from the tenement it felt like freedom, a completely other world. There were paths and trees and lakes and even horses, now that the war was over. Don once saw a woman in narrow, beige pants and a black velvet hat riding a horse along a trail in the park. He was astounded as he had never seen a real horse. He stood, transfixed, watching the woman ride by on this massive, beautiful animal. And in New York! Where did the horse live, when it wasn't being ridden in the park?

If he thought of it, Don would bring his sketchbook and a pencil with him and sit in the sun along the walking path, drawing the grass and trees or a scurrying squirrel. On one of these walks, in the early spring, he came upon the ominous-looking Belvedere Castle. Why, Don wondered, was there a castle in Central Park? This discovery enchanted him. He would sit on the bench along the path and stare at the castle. He imagined all sorts of scenarios: an evil king living inside, with his minions running around and doing his dirty work for him. Was there a beautiful, young princess longing to get out? Perhaps there was a stable and horses on the other side?

One grey Saturday afternoon, Don decided to

find out. Walking along the narrow winding paths, he made his way up the hill to the other side of the castle. He was so caught up in his quest to see if there was a stable, that he hadn't noticed the sky had turned a lead grey.

When he got to the top of the hill what he found was not a stable with horses but a girl in her teenage years, with bobbed white blond hair and extremely red lipstick, singing as she skipped down the path on the other side of the hill. The song sounded vaguely familiar to Don, but he could not quite place it. As she skipped, she tossed something in the air that fell along the path. Was it paper? Confetti? As Don followed her, he became incredulous. Singles, five- and ten-dollar bills, flew out of her hands as if she was tossing crumbs to birds.

At this moment, Don heard an almost deafening thunderclap, a gust of wind accosted him, and it started to rain. "Miss!" he called. "Are these yours?" he ran after the girl, while trying to pick up the fallen money from the ground.

The girl continued to sing, very loudly, swaying from side to side and seemingly oblivious to Don's protests. Wet, yet stunned, Don continued to peel the now slick bills off the ground. When he couldn't find any more, he bunched them up and shoved them in his pants pocket. He then tried to catch up with the young woman, who was just ahead of him on the path, making her way down the hill on the other side of the castle.

"Miss!" Don called again, finally catching up

with her. Seeing that she still did not respond he caught up with, then ran in front of her so that she had to stop, as there was nowhere to go. "Miss, are these yours?" Don demanded. "Did you lose them?" He pulled out some of the wadded-up bills from his pocket and showed them to her.

The girl stared at Don, and pushed her wet hair, which had fallen in front of her eyes, away. She continued to list from side to side, while still singing the song, only not as loudly as before. She looked down at Don's hand and then took him in.

"Sure, they're mine," she said. "Or they *were*. I don't want 'em anymore. You want 'em? You can have 'em. And what's more? I stole 'em!" She looked Don in the eye as she said this. "There! How do you like that?!"

Don was incredulous. He didn't know how to respond. He simply stared at her while the rain dripped down the side of his face, his neck, and underneath his shirt.

"Yup," the girl continued. "I took 'em from the old man. He's a louse, and a cheat. He's a two-timer and he deserves everything he gets!" The young woman was listing from side to side as she spoke. Don wondered whether she was drunk.

He fished out one of the bills from his pocket. "Are you sure you don't want them back?" Don asked, holding the bill towards her.

"What's wrong with you?" the girl yelled at Don. "Didn't you hear me? I don't want 'em! They're yours, for all I care!"

"Did you take these from your father?" Don asked.

"He's not my *father!*" the girl cried bitterly. "He's my mother's *boyfriend*" she said, almost singing the word mockingly. "And now he's cheating on my mother. I found out. And I knew where he hid his money." She paused. "So, I just decided to help myself. He's not gonna miss it. Besides, he's loaded, the rat!"

Don looked at her, trying to take in the whole picture. He wasn't good at judging age, but he figured she was probably around thirteen years old. She was wearing a navy blue coat with shiny brass buttons, which strongly contrasted her white-blonde hair, and a dress in a pale blue floral print underneath. In the rain, Don could smell the scent of wet wool emanating from her coat.

"Miss, aren't you going to get in trouble when he discovers the money is missing?" Don asked. He couldn't quite grasp the amount of money the girl had gotten a hold of.

For the first time, the girl looked at Don without listing from side to side. She no longer seemed drunk. "What's it to you?" she asked, pointing her index finger at Don.

"Nothing, only I can't keep your money. Here." Don started taking the wadded-up bills from his pocket to hand back to her. "And I'd hate to think you'd get in trouble when you get home."

"I never heard of such a thing," the girl cried, as she reluctantly took the money back from Don.

"Here he gets free money, and he wants to return it. To a dirty, rotten, no good—"

"I know what you mean," said Don. "From what you're telling me he doesn't sound like a good guy. But I also don't think you should steal from him. That's not the answer."

"'Not the answer?!'" the girl mimicked. "Then what *is* the answer, my friend? Say, what's your name, anyway. I mean, after all, if I'm gonna meet such a chump, I oughta know what his name is."

"My name's Don," he replied. "What's yours?"

"Martha," she said.

"Well, Martha, it's very nice to meet you," said Don. The rain had slowed down. "Would you like me to walk you out of the park?" Don asked.

Martha looked at Don and tried to make him out. "You're a funny one, aren't you?" She paused. "Sure, you can walk me out of the park." They proceeded down the path that led to the exit at West 81st Street and Central Park West.

As they walked away together from the castle, Don turned to Martha. "I know you think I'm nuts, but I think you should return the money to your mother's boyfriend. He did a bad thing—I completely agree—but you shouldn't steal. That's not right either."

"Really?" Martha asked. "You think I oughta return the money? That's just the craziest thing I've ever heard." She looked Don straight in the eye.

"I know," said Don. "But you'll still get in trouble when he finds out. Besides, it's the right thing to do."

"Now, wait a minute," said Martha. "Let me ask *you* a question. If you were in my place and you kept the money, what would *you* do with it?

"Hmmm," Don mulled. "That's a really tough one. First of all, there's no way I could get away with keeping that kind of money because my mother would find out. Either I'd hide it, or I'd spend it, but either way, I know she would find out that I had stolen it. I do odd jobs around the neighborhood and make a little pocket change, but I've never had this kind of money. She'd know immediately."

"Gee, I wish I had a job," said Martha. "I get an allowance and that's okay, but I'd like to work, too."

"Well, if you ask me," Don said. "I think you should return the money. You should earn it instead of taking it. You could find some kind of job."

"Hmmm . . ." Martha mused. "Return the money . . . that's just about the craziest thing I ever heard of. Then she stopped and looked at Don. "You could have something, though. Maybe I *can* find some kind of job. I guess I could babysit some of those brats in my building . . ."

Don laughed. "Sure! There ya' go . . ."

By this point, Martha and Don were nearing the exit from the park. "Well," Martha said, turning to Don, "you're the strangest boy I ever met, but I enjoyed talking to you. Also . . ." she looked down at her shoes" I guess I should thank you."

"Well, don't thank me yet," said Don, smiling. "You might still get in trouble."

"Yup, I might," Martha said. "But I guess you're

right. I'd get in worse trouble if I didn't return the money. I live across the street there," she said, turning her head towards a fancy apartment building on the other side of Central Park West, "so I guess I should say goodbye."

"Goodbye, Martha," said Don.

"Goodbye, Don," said Martha.

Don watched Martha as she turned around and crossed Central Park West, then entered the apartment building on the opposite side of the street where a doorman greeted her at the entrance. Don observed what a different life Martha must live. He looked up at the building, then back down, and counted the twelve floors from the street to the top. He wondered which of those windows Martha lived in. Did her room face the park? What a thing that would be, Don thought, to have a view of Central Park. He turned around and headed back down the path to go home.

The rain had stopped, and the sun was trying to show itself through the clouds. As Don continued walking, he thought about Martha and marveled at the events of this afternoon.

If someone asked him what had just happened, how exactly would he explain it? He didn't think he could. One thing he could do is think about all that cash and the massive amount of art supplies he could have bought with it.

CHAPTER SEVEN

1957

After saying goodbye to Ruth in Chicago, Don picked up his backpack and headed into the brightly-colored Greyhound bus station.

Looking at the schedule board he saw that he had an hour to kill before boarding his next bus for Minneapolis. He was stiff, hungry, and tired. Walking over to one of the black and chrome benches, he sat down and planned his next ten minutes. First, he needed to find the men's room.

When he entered it, Don went into a stall, unbuttoned his shirt, and examined his chest. A red rash was making its way up from his belly, where the fishing vest began. In some parts small, white blisters were beginning to appear. He had unzipped the fishing vest and began fanning himself with it. The air felt good.

Next, he had to get some hot black coffee since he had polished off what was left in the Thermos long ago.

Then he would take a walk. It would be good

to move his body after all those hours of sitting on the bus. As he was contemplating getting up to find a coffee shop, he saw a sign for a bag check counter. That's what he would do, he would check his backpack for an hour so that he could take a walk unburdened by luggage.

The man at the counter gave him a red cardboard ticket with the number 25 on it. Don looked at the number and a smile crossed his face. He pocketed the ticket and walked across the lobby. He hadn't felt that free in days. As he walked toward the station entrance, he remembered Chicago was known as the Windy City. It was going to be bracingly cold when he walked out that door. Maybe a walk wasn't such a good idea after all.

Against all better judgment, Don pulled open the door and was smacked by an icy blast of air. *Oh, well,* he thought, as he headed into the wind. *I need to move my legs.* Turning right, Don walked down a street that was surrounded by large office buildings and a grand hotel. Looking in, he saw a carpeted lobby with palm trees and couches and hotel staff dressed in caps and white gloves. Don pushed on the revolving door and as he emerged on the other side the door man said, "Welcome to the Hotel Stevens."

Inside, Don wasn't sure what he should do next. He was fascinated by the warm and cozy look of the hotel, but he knew loiterers would be removed on the spot, so he decided to make a call. "Where can I find a telephone, please?" he asked the doorman.

"Down that hallway, sir, to your left, around the

corner," the man said, pointing his white-gloved finger in that direction.

"Thank you," Don responded, thinking he had never been called "sir" before.

"No trouble at all, sir." Don was struck by the man's cheerful demeanor. *Gee, wouldn't it be nice to get a warm room here rather than get on another bus?* Don thought. He could take a hot bath, and order Room Service. He had always fantasized about ordering Room Service, the way they did in the movies.

Don sank into the seat in the telephone booth and slid the door shut. Pulling up and opening the thick telephone directory, he looked for Marshall Field's Department Store. "WA-bash 2–4900," Don said out loud, as he held his finger over the entry. Before making the call, he rehearsed to himself what he would say.

Don reached into his pocket and found the ten cents to place the call.

"Hello?" he asked the operator who had answered at Marshall Field's. "I'm looking for an employee named Ruth . . . uh . . ." Don thought, "Morgan! That's her name—Ruth Morgan. She works in Day Wear. Can you tell me when she is expected at work next? Yes, I'll hold . . ." Don cradled the phone as he pulled a small notebook and pencil from his jacket pocket. He tapped his fingers on the side of the telephone as he waited for a response. "She works Mondays through Fridays? Thank you so much for your help, ma'am."

Don hung up the receiver and slid open the door. He looked at his watch. Another forty-five minutes before he had to be at the bus. He turned around and walked back through the lobby, giving it a wistful nod as he prepared himself for the cold. "Have a nice evening, sir," the same doorman said to him as he pushed the revolving door for him.

Heading back to the Greyhound station Don thought it was time to get that cup of coffee; inside the lobby he headed to Stineway Drug on the right side and took a seat at the curvy, pale pink Formica counter.

"What can I get you, son?" asked the white-capped waiter who put out a napkin, fork, knife, and spoon at Don's place.

"Coffee, please—black—a chicken salad sandwich, and a piece of apple pie," Don replied.

"Comin' right up," the waiter said, writing down his request with a pencil on a small order pad.

"Twenty-five" . . . Don thought, taking the bag check ticket out of his pocket, examining it in his hand. It had to be that number, Don laughed to himself, thinking about Mr. Stephanich, a patron at the bar and his love of the number twenty-five. Mr. Stephanich always came in on Fridays and handed Don thirty-five cents, ten for his Pabst Blue Ribbon and twenty-five "for the house," he would say, winking at Velma.

"Ma," Don said to her, curious about the transaction that had just taken place. "He gave me too much money."

"You don't worry about too much, Dontchik, you just give to me the money," Velma replied.

Confused, Don handed her the change, which she rang up in the silver register at the back of the bar, before going back to serve the patrons.

That same evening, Mrs. Florek handed Don a one-dollar bill and asked for fifty cents in change. Don did the math: fifteen cents for her vodka and an additional thirty-five cents. "You give it your mother," Mrs. Florek said. Don rang up the register and placed the change in the drawer, trying to understand why Mrs. Florek would pay more for her drink than she needed to. Especially since none of the patrons of the bar had money to spare.

The next week, on a rainy Thursday evening, Don was wiping down the bar, right before opening time, when Mr. Schein knocked on the door.

"Hello, Mr. Schein," said Don. "We'll be open in ten minutes."

"Yes, yes, actually, I'm on my way home," said Mr. Schein "My wife has a bad cold. Could you give this to your mother, please?" and he pulled a small manila envelope from the interior pocket of his overcoat and handed it to Don. She's expecting this."

"Sure, okay," said Don. "I'll make sure she gets this. I hope Mrs. Schein feels better" he said, as he took the envelope, closed the door, and locked it after Mr. Schein left.

As Don carried the envelope to the back room, where Velma was seated at her desk with her eyes closed—she sometimes did this for about ten minutes before the bar opened—he noticed that the envelope Mr. Schein had handed him was not completely sealed. As he knocked on the door he looked down and saw several dollars visible through the opening.

"Yes?" Velma asked, sleepily.

"Ma, Mr. Schein came by and asked me to give this to you," Don said, opening the door and handing the envelope to Velma.

"Ah, yes, thank you, Dontchik," Velma said, taking the envelope from him and placing it on the desk. She then proceeded to open the bottom desk drawer on the right and produce a small grey metal lock box, which she placed on the desk. Choosing a miniature key from the chain she wore around her neck, she inserted it into the lock on the side of the box, opened it, and placed Mr. Schein's envelope inside. She then closed the box, locked it, and replaced the box in the drawer again.

"Ma," Don asked, stepping closer to the desk. "Why was Mr. Schein giving you money?"

Velma paused. "Dontchik," Velma turned and looked at him. "You ask so many questions," she said, standing up and running her fingers through his hair. "*So* many questions, my Dontchik, he asks," she repeated,

"But Ma, why?" Don persisted. "Why was he giving you money?"

Velma, starting to get exasperated, finally answered. "Okay, you ask, I tell. He borrow money from me, and he return. So, now you know!"

"He borrowed money from you?" Don asked. "Why?"

"Ach . . ." Velma responded, pointing to the watch she wore on her left wrist. "You look what time it is. We go open door, Dontchik."

CHAPTER EIGHT

1947

Don loved staring at the stained glass windows in the 84th Street subway station.

It was a sunny Saturday afternoon in April, and he had decided he wanted to ride the train to see where all the people went when they rode by the apartment window. He had wanted to do this for a very long time.

The stained glass was made up of a pattern that was dark red, green, and blue, and when he looked through the window from the other side everything looked like a multi-faceted jewel. Don imagined he was in a medieval kingdom, and he was looking at all his subjects, to whom he was about to give an edict, standing in line, waiting for their moment with him on the platform of the Third Avenue El.

He figured he would take the train almost to the end of the line, Chatham Square, and see what was there. He had an idea that there was a whole other world downtown, with people and places completely different from Yorkville.

The train rattled in, and Don boarded, excited to find a seat by a window. As he settled in, he looked around. There was an older man with grey hair sitting in the corner seat, asleep and snoring, with his right hand holding something in his left breast pocket. Don wondered what it was, as he watched him list from side to side almost in concert with the movements of the train.

At one point the man almost fell over, immediately waking up and looking confusedly around him. Pulling a flat bottle from the pocket of his worn wool jacket, he unscrewed the top, took a long swig and replaced the cap and bottle in his pocket again. Don wondered what he was drinking. He could not see the label. Was it something Velma served at the bar? It must have been either vodka or gin because the liquid inside the bottle was clear.

At 59th Street a young woman got on and sat down directly across from Don. She was beautiful, with long dark hair and warm brown eyes. She opened her purse and pulled out a compact and lipstick and proceeded to apply the deep red color to her full lips. She also checked her hair, running her fingers through it like a comb. Don wondered where she was going. He tried not to stare but he could not take his eyes off her.

At 42nd Street, a man got on with a little boy. The man was wearing a navy blue pin striped suit, and the boy also had a dark blue suit on with short pants. It looked like they were going somewhere special. They found a seat and the boy immediately turned around and rose up on his knees to look out the window. Don remembered doing that with Velma when he was little and they went shopping at S. Klein, in Union Square, but Velma would not let him turn around to look out the window. "Dontchik, you sit down," she told him, leaving Don to wonder what the big deal was about looking out the window.

Don leaned back and closed his eyes and listened to the sound of the train as it made its way down Third Avenue. It was strange, listening to this sound here and not from the inside of the apartment. It was a different sound, much louder, and he liked the way he could feel the vibrations in his body as the train rattled over the tracks.

Don didn't realize he had fallen asleep. When he woke up, he looked around and didn't recognize where he was. The buildings were not familiar to him and when he looked down at the street below, he did not see any landmarks that he knew. Suddenly Don became concerned that he may have gone too far; perhaps this adventure wasn't a good idea, after all. He started to feel his heartbeat escalate and he wasn't quite sure what he should do. At that moment, he noticed that someone had left a newspaper, folded up on the wicker seat next to him. Don picked it up and saw that the comics sheet was still intact. He looked for *Archie* and began reading.

Before he knew it, the announcement came for Chatham Square. Don looked up and felt better. His heart wasn't racing anymore. Stepping off the train, he looked around and decided to follow the small crowd of passengers to the left and down the steps. When he got to the bottom of the stairs, he found a trash bin and threw out the newspaper. He then looked around and realized he must be near Chinatown because many of the signs were not in English.

As he exited the station Don began walking to the left and decided to turn onto a little street that curved around called Doyers. Tiny restaurants and laundry shops lined the sidewalks and the smells made Don suddenly realize he was hungry. He decided he would get something to eat.

Walking up to one of the windows he looked at the menu and decided to go inside and order an egg roll. While he waited, he looked around, watching the people who walked by. The men and women looked like they were in a rush to get somewhere. *Where?* Don wondered. After the woman behind the counter handed him a steaming egg roll in a wax paper bag, Don continued to walk along Doyers until it circled over to Pell. The egg roll was hot, still too hot to eat, so Don walked and looked around, completely taken with all the unfamiliar colors and sounds of the neighborhood: men sitting on wooden crates, cleaning fish and women at stands selling vegetables. Don listened to the language spoken and wished he could understand some of the words.

From Pell, Don turned right on Mott and made his way to Canal, where he crossed the street with the crowd. On the other side of Canal, Mott continued into Little Italy. Now, the signs were understandable and advertised pasta, cheese, and pastries. Here older men sat on stoops and smoked cigars while women pushed baby carriages and children played on the sidewalks. By this point Don had finished his egg roll and was thinking he'd like to get something sweet.

On Grand Street, Don turned left and walked by a bakery called Ferrara. He stopped and looked at all the luscious-looking baked goods in the window. He decided to go inside where he stood transfixed as a woman behind the counter filled cannoli shells with a ricotta filling studded with chocolate chips. Don ordered one, and watched as the woman delicately picked it up in wax paper from the display case and placed it in a white paper bag. After paying for it and walking out the door, Don spotted a bench outside. *Perfect,* he thought, and sat down to eat his cannoli while looking at the people passing by. *Where are they all going?* Don wondered.

Just as he was finishing his last bit of gooey cream and crunchy shell, he felt a raindrop on the tip of his nose. Looking up, he saw that the sky had turned a dark slate grey. He was wearing a thin cotton shirt and had no umbrella. What was he going to do? Bunching up the paper that the Cannoli had come in and throwing it back in the paper bag, Don got up and walked over to the garbage can on the corner to throw the bag away.

As he stood there, contemplating the rain that now felt thicker and heavier, Don realized his downtown adventure was coming to an end. He had no umbrella, he would probably get soaked, then when he got home, he would have Velma to contend with.

Nothing was worse, he had learned from long, hard experience, than coming home soaked. "You catch cold!" Velma would cry out, running for a towel, change of clothes, and hot tea. Then he would sit at the kitchen table with the towel around his neck, drinking the tea while Velma rapidly dried his hair, waiting for the whole ordeal to be over.

What next? Don thought, as he looked around, trying to figure out how to proceed. He had to make it back to the subway or he had to wait out the rain before getting back home. He felt around in his pants pocket and found some change—not enough, though, to go back and buy another treat at Ferrara. The only thing to do, Don decided, was find a newspaper to shelter himself as best he could from the rain. That way he could make a break back to the Chatham Square station.

Looking down, he found a folded-up newspaper in the trash can. *Just my luck!* Don thought, as he took it out, unfolded it enough so that it would form a triangle over his head. Holding it with both hands in this manner he started making his way back down Mott Street to the Chatham Square station.

CHAPTER NINE

1957

In Minneapolis, Don was followed by a short man with mean eyes.

After he got off the bus he stopped at Snyder's Drug and ordered a hot turkey sandwich and coffee. While he was eating the man sat down on the stool next to his right and started to make conversation. He was dark haired and wore a navy blue utility jacket with dark grey pants.

"Good sandwich, huh?" the man said. Don could smell his cigarette-laced breath.

"Yup, sure is," Don responded, hoping the man would go away.

"They don't make a better turkey sandwich anywhere," the man continued.

"Uh, huh." Don hoped the man would stop talking. He was exhausted from the endless hours on the bus, and he just wanted to eat his sandwich and drink his coffee. He already missed his conversation with Ruth, and talking with a stranger at a lunch counter would certainly not make up for it.

"Say, you from around here?" the man asked, persisting.

"What's it to you?" Don was beginning to get irritated.

"Oh, nothing at all. It's just I'm trying to recruit some folks for a job."

"No, thanks," said Don, wiping his mouth with his napkin. "I've already got a job." Instead of quietly eating his sandwich, Don had to devise a plan to get the man off his back.

"Do you really? What line of work you in, son?" Don felt the man leaning in on him.

"Listen," said Don turning to the man, "I don't mean to rain on your parade, but I'm just trying to finish up my meal if you don't mind."

Don considered saying he was about to catch another bus, but he thought better of it. He drank his last sip of coffee and wiped his mouth with his napkin. Standing up, he reached into his pocket to take out a dollar bill but pulled out a five instead. He was careful about having a roll of small bills with singles in his jeans pocket at all times but he must have forgotten to make change and have some available. He was reluctant to let the man see the large bill.

Don walked over to the register by the front door and handed the cashier the check his waitress had given him and the five-dollar bill. He was about to turn back to leave the waitress her tip at the counter when he remembered that the man was still there. He didn't want to have any more interactions with him if he could avoid it.

"Hot turkey sandwich and coffee," the cashier said, as she rang up his tab at the register. "That'll be ninety-five cents."

"Listen," Don said, leaning in to speak with the cashier without being heard, "will you do me a favor and leave this tip for the waitress that served me, please?"

"Sure, I'd be happy to," she said. Don noticed she was young, had strawberry blond hair, and wore bright red lipstick.

"Thanks. I appreciate that," he said and headed for the door.

On Hawthorne, Don turned right and stayed close to the buildings to keep out of the wind. As he proceeded down the street, he got the sense that he was being followed by the man. At first, Don thought if he walked rapidly in the cold, he could shake him. After all, who wanted to follow someone in the bitter cold? After walking a few blocks at a rapid pace, though, Don stopped in front of a men's clothing store window and turned slightly to his right and saw the man coming down the block.

Continuing down the street, he crossed North 10th and hoped to lose the man while quickly making it across before the traffic light turned red. As he made it back up onto the curb and continued to walk, he got the sense that he still had not lost the man, which was confirmed when he stopped and turned around, bluntly staring ahead as the man continued to walk down the street toward him.

Finally, Don decided that it was time to take action and get help. Not sure what he should do to lose him, he continued to walk until he got to the corner of Hawthorne and North 11th, where he decided to duck into a newsstand in the Hotel Belvedere. Picking up a paper, he gave the counter man a dime and perused the sports section. While doing so, he kept his eyes peeled for the man to see if he was coming from the left-hand side of the street. When he spied him, he decided to approach the bellhop in the lobby and find out if there was a police station in the area. He really didn't want to resort to calling the cops, but he was starting to see that he may not have a choice.

"Excuse me," he said to the man. "Where is the nearest police station?" he asked in a louder-than-usual voice, looking around to see if the man could hear him.

"Down the street and to the right on Hennepin," the bell man said.

"Great. Thank you very much," Don said, headed in that direction. When he got to the corner of Hennepin, he made a quick turn, thinking about whether he would actually walk into the police station or whether he would just stand outside, hoping that he could just shake the man off before involving the cops.

Suddenly, it dawned on him that he had to catch his connecting bus. Approaching the police station, Don decided he would stop and looked at his watch, then walk up the stairs to the front door of the precinct and look back. If he saw the man, he would go in. If he didn't, he would head back to the bus station.

Don checked his watch and headed up the stairs. When he turned around, the man was gone.

CHAPTER TEN

1949

Fridays were laundry day.

Velma would wash twelve-year-old Don's shirts and pants in the white enamel double kitchen sink, soaking them in the hot, soapy water on the left and rinsing them in the cooler water on the right. When she was done, she would drain both sinks and wring out the clothing as best she could to get the excess water out, then place the wet laundry over towels in a wicker basket.

"Dontchick, you take upstairs now," Velma would call, and Don would take his cue to carry the heavy laundry basket up the three flights of stairs to the roof. In the warmer months, this gave Don time to be alone with his thoughts, enjoying the warmth of the sun on his face. In the colder months, it was a challenge to hang the cold, wet laundry while wearing gloves. He had to be done before 4:30 when the sun set.

One warm March afternoon, Don had just started hanging a pair of pants. When he reached down into the basket to grab a clothespin the roof door opened. A girl in a black coat with long, dark hair in two braids down her back carried a basket of her own. She brought it over to the line where Don was hanging his shirts.

"Hello," she said, as she put the basket down.

"Hello," said Don.

The girl took out a white blouse from the basket and started hanging it on the line.

"My name's Allison," she said. "I just moved in on the third floor."

"Oh, I'm Don," he replied. "I live on the second floor."

"It's so warm out today. Maybe spring will come soon," Allison said.

"Yes," Don said, looking up at the sky.

"How long have you been living here?"

"Oh, my whole life," Don answered. "Where did you live before you moved here?"

"We lived on the Lower East Side, but my mother needed to be closer to her family. My grandmother isn't well, and she needs my mother's help."

"Oh, I see," Don said.

"I go over and help her in the afternoons when I come home from school sometimes. She also likes it when I read to her. I see you have to help your mother, too," she said, looking down at Don's laundry basket.

"Yes, Friday is laundry day," he replied.

"That's funny. It's laundry day at my house, too!" Allison said and smiled at Don.

"I don't have any grandparents here," Don said, as he started to hang his pants.

"Here?" Allison responded.

"No, they're all in the old country," Don said, clipping the pants with the clothes pin. "We don't hear from them much."

"Where is that?" asked Allison.

"Russia," said Don.

"Oh, my family is from Ireland."

"Ah," Don responded.

"My grandfather died a couple of years ago and my grandmother is on her own now. That's why she needs my mother's help," Allison said, as she hung a dress with small red flowers on it.

"I wish I knew my grandparents," said Don. "It's just me and my mother."

"Where is your father?" Allison asked.

"Oh, he died a long time ago. I never met him."

"I'm sorry," Allison said. "It must be hard, not having a father."

"Yeah," Don said, looking at the building across Third Avenue. "I wish I knew him," said Don.

"My dad sings," Allison said, hanging another white blouse on the line.

"He sings?" Don asked, as he pulled out another pair of pants from the basket.

"Yes, he sings all the time," Allison replied.

"What does he like to sing?" asked Don, as he reached down for a clothespin.

"Oh, my goodness, every Irish song ever written!" Allison said, laughing. "I feel bad for saying this but sometimes I wish he would just stop singing!"

"Does your mom like it when your dad sings?" Don asked. By this point he had hung his last pair of pants.

"Most of the time, she doesn't mind it," Allison responded, "but sometimes you can see that it gets on her nerves. There's never any peace!" Allison paused. "Well, I guess I'd better be going now," she said, as she hung the last pillowcase on the line.

"Sure. Me too," said Don as he hurried to clip his last shirt on the line.

As they approached the heavy metal door that led to the stairwell, Don said, "Here, let me get that for you," as he put down his empty basket in order to open the door for Allison.

"Thank you, Don," said Allison. "It was nice meeting you."

"It was nice meeting you, too," Don said, as she walked through the door, carrying her own basket.

He held the door with his foot while he reached down and picked up his basket, letting the door close behind him.

CHAPTER ELEVEN

1957

By the time Don got off at the Greyhound station in Billings, his body felt like a board. All his limbs ached from being on a bus for three days. He had a headache and he felt slightly chilled. It occurred to him that he might be getting a cold.

He reached into his jacket pocket to pull out what was now a handkerchief badly in need of laundering. The sun was shining, though, and in the distance over the buildings of downtown Billings, Don could see mountains. The air was fresh and as he breathed it in, he started to feel just a little bit better.

Outside the station on North 4th Don found a lunch counter where he could make a phone call. In the telephone booth at the back, he dialed a number and waited.

"Hello, Sergei? . . . Yes, I'm in Billings, my bus just got in . . . All right, but I'm not feeling well . . . I'm not sure but I may be coming down with a cold . . . Yes, you're right, just in time . . . what is the address for Ivan? . . . Just a second, let me get a pencil and write it down." Don reached into his jacket pocket to pull out a small notebook and lead pencil. "All right, I'm ready . . . Ivan Melik . . . La Grange apartments . . . Yes, I'll call him now and tell him I've arrived . . . Yes, I'll say hello to Velma. Hi, Ma . . . Yes, I'm fine, just tired . . . No, Ma, I'm not sick, just a bit stuffy . . . Okay, Ma, I'll have Ivan make me strong black tea . . . I have to call him now, Ma . . . Goodbye."

Don hung up and headed to the counter. "Coffee and a slice of apple pie, please," he said to the waitress. "Say, can you tell me how far the La Grange apartments are from here?" he asked her.

"The La Grange?" she asked, as she put a cup and saucer down on the counter, then poured black coffee from a glass carafe into it. "Oh, not far. You can walk there in ten minutes," she said. "Or, if it's too cold, you can get a cab at the corner of 4th; the La Grange is on the corner of North Broadway and 4th." She turned around to retrieve the apple pie from the metal and glass cooler over the back counter.

"Thanks, I appreciate that," Don said.

"Say, you're not from around here, are you?" the waitress said, placing the slice of pie in front of Don.

"No, just visiting," Don responded. Don was too tired to engage in any more conversations about being from New York City and what he was doing in Montana.

Luckily, an older man, dressed in denim coveralls, a wool jacket and felt hat, sat down next to Don and ordered coffee and pulled out a folded copy of the Billings Gazette from his back pocket.

Don took his last swig of coffee and said to the waitress, "Well, thanks for the pie." He smiled as he picked up the tab and kneeled down to pick up his backpack.

"Anytime," the waitress said, handing Don his change. "C'mon back and see us if you're in town for a while. We don't get a lot of out-of-towners here."

"Sure, I'll do that," Don said as he placed some coins on the counter and headed back out the door, turning left on North 4th Avenue. Billings was a low town, with buildings no more than a few stories high. How different it was from New York. Don could see the sky here, which, with its oversized white clouds, seemed enormous to him. He stopped and stared, trying to take it all in. Finally, he realized he was going to look odd to the locals, just standing there and looking at the sky, so he continued walking down the street.

At the corner, he saw several taxis and climbed into the first one. "Can you take me to the La Grange apartments, please?"

"Sure," said the cabbie. They rode in silence for a few minutes. Then: "You from out of town?"

"Yup. From New York State," he lied, but not really. "Visiting family."

"Gotcha," said the cabbie. "Ever been to the big city?" he asked.

"Nah, always wanted to though," Don said. "Maybe someday . . ." he looked out the window, ready to be at his destination.

"All right. Here were are—La Grange Apartments," the driver said, slowing down in front of a four-story building from the turn of the century. "That'll be seventy-five cents."

"Thanks," said Don. "Keep the change."

"You betcha. Thanks!"

In front of the La Grange, Don looked at the three-floor, brick building, which reminded him a little of the ones in Yorkville. He then took a breath before walking up to the entrance and pushing open the door.

"Room ten, please," Don said to the clerk behind the front desk.

"Room ten," repeated the clerk, "down the hall and to the right."

"Thanks," said Don, heading in that direction.

When he got to the door, he knocked and waited. Eventually, it was opened by a middle-aged man, around forty-five, with brown hair combed back and warm green eyes. He wore dark horn-rimmed glasses.

"Don!" Ivan proclaimed, when he opened the door. He gave Don a warm hug. "Come in, come in!"

"Hello," Don said, awkwardly hugging Ivan back. He stepped inside the hallway and put down his backpack.

"My goodness, Don, you're a man!" Ivan said, looking him up and down. "How did this happen?

The last time I saw you was at Velma's. You were just a boy helping behind the bar."

"Yes," Don said, "that was right before you and Nina moved, right?"

"That's right," said Ivan, "but come in and sit down. We don't have to stand in the hallway. Let me take your jacket."

"Would you mind if I wash up first?" Don asked.

"No, of course not! Ivan answered. "The bathroom is right there," and he pointed to the door in the hallway.

Don went into the bathroom and closed the door. He looked in the mirror over the sink. He was pale and there were massive bags beneath his eyes. *Wow,* he thought, *I look like hell. I really do need to sleep.*

Taking off his jacket, Don unbuttoned his shirt and took it off so he could remove the vest, which he reversed so that the money could not be seen and rolled it up, placing it on the floor. Then he leaned over the sink and turned on both faucets, running a washcloth he found on the towel rack through the hot and cold water. He then covered his face with the washcloth and breathed in. It felt good. He wished he could do this for the next hour.

After washing his hands, as well, Don picked up the jacket and vest off the floor and opened the bathroom door a crack to see where Ivan was. When he didn't see him, he quickly walked back into the room, placing the vest in his backpack, which he had left on the floor in the hallway.

Ivan then came out of the kitchen and motioned Don to the grey sofa in the living room. Don sat down and looked around. In addition to the small living room, there was a kitchenette to the right, and a hallway with the bathroom and a bedroom to the left.

The living room was square, with an overstuffed armchair in the corner and matching hassock. In the other corner, there was a small dining table with two chairs, a white tablecloth, a set of salt-and-pepper shakers and a small glass carafe.

"Don, I've put on the water for tea. Would you like a cup?"

"Yes, that would be great. Thank you," Don responded.

"Of course," Ivan said. He retreated into the kitchen after he heard the kettle whistling on the electric stove.

"How was the trip, Don?" Ivan asked, as he spooned loose tea leaves into a round brown tea pot. "Was the bus ride long?"

"Yes, very long," Don responded from the living room. "To be honest, I'm actually not feeling very well," he continued. "I feel like I may be coming down with a cold."

"Oh, no! I am so sorry to hear that," Ivan responded, bringing the kettle to the table "but somehow not surprised, sitting on a bus for all that time. After tea and a meal, you will sleep!"

"Gee, thank you," said Don, "I don't want to put you out."

"Nonsense," Ivan said, bringing the tea pot to the table. You can sleep in my room, or, if you prefer, on the couch. He returned to the kitchen to fetch cups, saucers, spoons, a small pitcher of cream and some golden butter cookies on a clear green plate.

"Come, let's sit and have some tea," Ivan said, as he placed the items on the table.

"Thank you," Don said, as he got up from the couch.

Ivan poured him a cup, motioning to the creamer and container of sugar. "After tea," Ivan said, "then, you go take a nap in my room. I can also give you some aspirin, as well." He handed Don his cup.

"Yes, thank you. Tea and a nap—that sounds really good," said Don, pouring some cream into his cup.

"So, tell me," said Ivan, "how was the trip?" He had poured himself a cup as well, and was now passing the plate of cookies toward Don. "Have a cookie," he said.

"The trip," Don said, leaning back and running his hand through his hair. "Wow. The trip was long. But it was okay, I guess. I met a nice woman on the way."

"Oh, yes? Tell me about her," said Ivan, smiling.

"Well, her name is Ruth, and she works at Marshall Field's in Chicago, as a dress model. She was returning from Cleveland, where her mother had just died."

"Oh, I am sorry to hear that," replied Ivan. "The loss of a parent is devastating."

"Yes, it must be terrible," Don continued. "When I was listening to her talk about it, I pictured how it would feel to lose Velma, and I just couldn't imagine. When she was sick that time, I was so worried about her."

"Yes, I know you were. We were all worried about her," said Ivan.

"You know," said Don, "it's funny, when I was sitting on the bus, I had so much time to think. Maybe too much time."

"Yes, I can understand that, said Ivan. "Too much time to sit is sometimes not a good thing."

"And I had this horrible thought," Don continued.

"What was that?" Ivan asked.

"What if Velma had died when she was sick that time? There were so many things we didn't say to each other."

"Ah, what things would those be?" asked Ivan.

"Well, to start with, what really happened to my father?" Don asked. "I mean, she always said he got sick and died before I was born. But she never talked about him, never told any stories. For that matter, she never talked about anything that happened when she was growing up. I don't know anything about her life in the old country."

"Yes, this is hard, Don," said Ivan.

"Why is it so hard?" asked Don. "I don't understand. Lots of families tell stories to their kids."

"Well, Don, you see, it is not so simple," said Ivan, who had gotten up to bring the teapot into the kitchen. At the stove, he refilled it with boiling water. Coming back to the table, he asked Don, "More tea?"

"Yes, please," Don replied, sliding his cup and saucer across the table.

"Velma, and Sergei, as well," Ivan continued, "suffered a lot of hardship in the old country. They had to leave the only home they knew, they lost family members under Stalin, and they had to start over in America. This is not easy. And it is even harder to talk about."

"Hmmm," said Don, "I never thought about it that way." He took a sip of his tea and reached for another cookie.

"I know people from the old country," said Ivan, "who simply won't talk about their past lives. They are here now, in the New World, as it were, and they don't feel comfortable reliving their history. If anything, I think they find it painful."

"I guess I always wanted our family to be like other families," said Don. "To tell stories. To share funny memories."

"Yes, I can certainly understand that," Ivan replied. "That is what one would think normal families do. But you see, Don, immigrant families really aren't like other families, are they? Their experience is so different from families who have been in America for generations."

"Yes, I see what you mean," Don replied. "I guess lots of kids from the neighborhood came from immigrant families."

"Yes, they did," answered Ivan. "But not all immigrant families are alike, either."

"That's right, isn't it?" asked Don. "I mean, I have a friend—Allison—she's Irish, or at least her family is. But they talk and laugh about a lot of family stories."

"Yes, the Irish are a different culture from the Slavs," said Ivan. "I met many Irish folk when we were living in New York and I found them to be very upbeat, almost cheerful. Slavs see the dark side of life much more."

"I couldn't agree more," said Don. He tried to suppress a yawn, covering his mouth with the back of his hand. "Well, if you don't mind, can I take you up on that offer to get a little shuteye before dinner?"

"Yes, of course!" said Ivan. "You must be exhausted, Don. Let me get an extra blanket for you" he said, standing up to go into the bedroom. "You want a couple of aspirin before you lie down?" he called out. "I've got some in the medicine cabinet."

"That would be great," Don said, as he realized his head was throbbing.

"Here, you go," said Ivan, returning from the bathroom and handing Don a small glass bottle of Bayer's aspirin. "Let me get you some water," he said, returning to the kitchen.

"Thank you," Don said, as Ivan came back and handed him the glass of water. He took two aspirin tablets from the bottle, placed them in the palm of his hand, then popped them in his mouth, followed by a sip of water.

"All right, the room is all set up for you, Don. You go and have a nice long rest," Ivan said.

"Thank you so much," said Don. "This is very kind of you."

"Nonsense," said Ivan. "You're like family to me. Now that my Nina is gone . . ." his voice trailed off. "Well, I am so happy to see you, Don!"

"Yes, me too," said Don, wanting to say something about Ivan's wife, but not knowing know how to respond. He picked up his backpack and retreated to Ivan's bedroom, closing the door behind him.

Don sat down on the bed and started to take off his shoes. He was so tired, and yet he had this feeling that he wouldn't be able to fall asleep just yet. Getting up once more, he walked over to his backpack and reached inside. The Spaldeen that he had packed was in the bottom of one of the interior compartments. He took it out and held it in his hand. Contemplating bouncing it on the floor, he looked down and saw that the floor was carpeted. Besides, what would Ivan think of a grown man bouncing a ball in his bedroom?

Don lay back on the bed and held the Spaldeen in his hand, turning it over and over, while he stared at the ceiling. He remembered the money in his backpack and wondered whether he had closed the flap shut. Maybe he had forgotten. The Spaldeen fell out of his hand and rolled onto the floor. Don closed his eyes, wondering whether he should get up and check the bag.

The door to the room quietly opened and Ivan walked in. He went over to Don's backpack and opened the flap, reaching inside for the vest. He removed it and sat down in the armchair, laying it out on his lap.

"There it is—all $12,000 of it," Don said, propping himself up on his elbow. "I'm thrilled to unload it."

"All right, I'll start counting," said Ivan, as he started to remove bundles of bills from the individual pockets in the vest.

Don sat up to watch him. It was the last thing he wanted to do. He wanted to go back to sleep. He felt achy and fatigued. Finally, Ivan finished counting and looked at Don, approvingly.

"It's all here," he said, as he started to place the bundles in a small brown leather suitcase.

"Excellent," said Don. "Mind if I go back to sleep? It's been awhile."

"Sure, go ahead. You just sleep for as long as you want. I'll turn off the light now," he said pushing the button on the switch plate and quietly closing the door.

"Thanks," said Don, as he rolled over and went back to sleep.

"Sleep for as long as you want . . . sleep for as long as you want . . ." Don repeated, as his head rolled from side to side.

"Don?" he heard a voice say. "Don, are you okay?" Don opened his eyes and looked up. Ivan was sitting on the side of the bed.

"I, uh . . ." Don stammered, rubbing his eyes with both hands.

"I think you were having a bad dream," said Ivan. "Do you want another cup of tea?" he asked.

"Yes," Don replied. "That would be great."

"Okay, you come out when you're ready," said Ivan, as he got up to leave the room.

Don sat up and looked around. Spotting his backpack on the floor, he noticed the flap was closed, just the way he had left it before he went to sleep.

He leaned his head back on the pillow and closed his eyes for another moment.

"What a dream," he murmured to himself.

CHAPTER TWELVE

1951

"It's funny," Allison was saying as she dipped her spoon into the dish, "I never used to like strawberry ice cream. Now I do." She smiled as she looked across the booth at the Lexington Candy Shop.

"That's interesting," said Don, as he played with the straw in his egg cream. "I never liked vanilla when I was little and now, I don't mind it so much." They both laughed. At age fourteen, Don was enjoying his memories of when he was small.

"Also, I've never had an egg cream," said Allison. "You're the first person I know who likes them. Most of my friends like ice cream sundaes.

"What?" Don responded. "Well, that's just a crime. Here, have a sip," Don offered, sliding his egg cream across the table to Allison.

Allison took a sip through the straw. "Oh! That's such a nifty flavor," she exclaimed. "Wait—is there really an egg in it?"

"Nah, there's no egg," Don explained. "I don't know why it's called that. What's in it is chocolate syrup, milk, and seltzer to make it all foamy at the top."

"I like it," said Allison. "I'm going to order one from now on. Then I can tell all my friends about it, too!"

"Can I get you kids anything else?" the waiter asked.

"Would you like something else?" Don asked Allison.

"No, thank you, I'm all right," said Allison.

"I guess we'll just take a check then," Don told the waiter.

"Alrighty, then!" replied the waiter. "One dish ice cream, one egg cream. Here ya go," and he ripped off the check from his pad and handed it to Don, who walked over to the cashier.

"Thank you for the ice cream, Don," said Allison.

"You're welcome," Don replied. "This was fun."

Don had really enjoyed getting to know Allison. They had become more and more friendly on their Friday afternoons on the roof, hanging laundry. Sometimes, on Saturdays, they would meet and go for a walk or get ice cream together. Don felt that he could talk to Allison, that he could say things to her that he could not tell other people. Allison seemed to listen. Everyone else just talked.

"Allison, can I ask you a question?" Don looked at her, as he held the door open when they walked out. It was a warm day in May and the sun shone brightly.

"Sure," she answered, as they turned left and started walking up East 83rd Street.

"It seems like your mother talks about her family, right? I mean she sees her mother regularly, and you do, too. Do they talk about things?"

"What kind of things do you mean?" Allison asked.

"I mean anything. Family things, people, other relatives," Don said. "I don't know, I guess I'm asking because we never talk about anything in my family. Maybe it's because it's just me and my mother but she never says anything about the old country or any of her family members. Sometimes, I'll hear her talking with my Uncle Sergei, but I don't understand Russian, so I don't know what they're talking about."

"Well, I guess we do talk in my family," said Allison. "I mean we Irish certainly know how to talk and tell stories." She laughed. "Somebody is always telling a story in my house."

"That's what I mean. We don't tell any stories in my family, especially funny ones," Don said. "What kind of funny stories do they tell, Allison?"

"Hmmm. Let me think," she replied. "Well, there's the story about the pig."

"The pig?" asked Don, as he started rolling up one of his shirt sleeves.

"Yes, you see," began Allison, "it seems there was this large pig that was always getting out of its pen on the farm—this was in County Mayo—and my grandparents were always running around trying to catch the pig."

"What happened next?" Don asked.

"One day," said Allison, "the pig disappeared, and my grandparents searched high and low, but they couldn't find it anywhere."

"Did they ever find it?" asked Don, who had rolled up both shirt sleeves by now.

"Yes—all the way on the other side of the valley—on another farm! It had found a lady pig friend to play with!" laughed Allison.

"That's a funny story!" said Don, who was also laughing, as he and Allison continued walking toward Fifth Avenue. "You see what I'm talking about? We never tell funny stories like that in my family."

"So, your mother doesn't tell stories at all?" Allison asked.

"Nope," said Don.

"What does she talk about?" asked Allison.

"That's just it," said Don. "She really doesn't talk much at all."

"Not at all?" asked Allison. "I mean, she must say something."

"Well, she'll say I'm a good boy, when I've helped her with the chores or when I work at the bar, and she'll talk to my Uncle Sergei and other adults, but I get the feeling that when it comes to me, she's not much of a talker."

"Well, I know this will sound strange to you but that would be a welcome relief in my family," said Allison. "I mean, I love them so much, but they are always talking. You cannot get them to stop!"

"Wow. What a difference that would be," said Don.

"What does your mother do when she's not working at the bar?" asked Allison.

"Oh, she shops for groceries and cleans the house. She does laundry. Sometimes, I guess to relax, she plays Solitaire."

"Solitaire?" asked Allison.

"Yeah, you know, the card game," Don replied.

"Oh, sure! Solitaire," Allison said.

"Yep, I'll come home sometimes, and she'll be sitting at the kitchen table, with her reading glasses on, playing Solitaire," Don explained.

"My grandmother plays that game, too. But she calls it something else. Do you ever play with your mother?" asked Allison.

"No, she never asks me," said Don

"Did you ever ask her?" asked Allison.

"No. I suppose I haven't," Don replied.

"Well, why don't you ask her sometime?" said Allison. "Maybe she doesn't know you're interested."

"Well, I guess I could," said Don. "Somehow it never occurred to me to ask her."

"Do you know how to play?" asked Allison.

"Not really," said Don.

"Well, I've played with my grandmother. You lay out six cards, face down, and one card face up at the end of the row; then you lay out five cards, face down, and one card face up. Then you do the same below, but the amount of cards gets smaller. You go along like that until you have an upside-down right triangle."

"Okay. What happens next?" asked Don.

"Well," Allison replied, "then, you try to lay the open cards below the king, down to the two. Black, then red, and vice versa. I can show you sometime."

"That would be fun," said Don. "But wait. It's not a game for two people."

"No, I guess not," said Allison. "But if I teach you then we have to play together!" said Allison.

"I would like that," said Don.

"Have you ever been there?" asked Allison, pointing at an imposing building that seemed to go on for blocks. They were standing in front of the Metropolitan Museum of Art.

"No," said Don. "What's that?"

"It's called the Metropolitan Museum of Art and if you've never been there, well, you are in for a treat. You can't imagine what they have in there."

"Really?" asked Don.

"Sure," said Allison. "There are paintings and sculptures and knights in armor and mummies and . . ."

"Holy smoke," said Don. "That's amazing!"

"And it goes on for days," said Allison. "I mean you can walk and walk, and it feels like it will never end. You can really get lost in there."

"Wow," said Don.

" 'Wow' is right," said Allison. "We could go sometime."

"That would be swell," said Don.

"And there's something else," Allison continued. "When I was there on a school trip last month I noticed another class of students and guess what they were doing?"

"What?" asked Don.

"They were sketching the knights in armor!" Allison replied.

"What?!" asked Don, incredulously.

"Yes, they were drawing the knights with lead pencils," answered Allison.

"Incredible," Don mused, wondering how amazing it would be to sit in the museum on a Saturday afternoon and draw a knight. Lately, he was spending more and more time on his drawings. One of his teachers at school, Mr. Ballard, had even encouraged him, telling Don he thought he had talent and that he should consider taking art classes outside of school. Don didn't know how he would come up with the money for such classes. He would have to take on more odd jobs after school and on the weekends. Then there was always the possibility that he could ask Sergei.

"I think we should go sometime," Allison was saying as they continued to walk south on Fifth Avenue.

"Huh?" Don asked.

"You seem far away, Don. Are you okay?" Allison said.

"Oh, I'm fine," Don replied.

"What were you thinking about?" she asked.

"Well," Don continued, "you mentioned the

museum and I was thinking how swell it would be to go inside and sketch. My art teacher, Mr. Ballard, has been commenting on my sketches at school and he told me last week he thinks I should take art classes outside of school."

"That's wonderful!" Allison proclaimed. "I wholeheartedly agree!"

"Thanks," Don said, smiling and taking Allison's hand. "That means the world to me."

"Say, there's something I want to show *you*," Don said, as they neared the 79th Street entrance to Central Park

"What's that?" asked Allison.

"You'll see," said Don, with a slight smile on his face.

They entered the park and began walking up the path. First, they walked under an arch where cars passed above, and then they came across a massive stone obelisk, that was shaped like a gigantic pin sticking up straight into the sky.

"What's this?" asked Allison, craning her neck to see the top.

"This," answered Don, "is called Cleopatra's Needle. Isn't it something else?"

"It sure is!" answered Allison. "Wow."

"Believed to be 3,000 years of age," a man was reading from a book to the woman who was standing next to him, "Cleopatra's Needle was a gift made to America from the Ottoman Viceroy of Egypt in 1881. It weighs 200 tons, is made of red granite, and measures sixty-nine feet. It was erected in approximately 1450 B.C. to commemorate the thirtieth anniversary of the reign of Pharaoh Thutmose."

Don and Allison listened to the man and gazed at the top. "I see why they call it a needle!" exclaimed Allison. "It gets narrower at the top. It really does look like a needle!"

"Sure does," said Don, as they continued to walk the path as it led up the hill. When they came to the clearing there were ball fields to the right, and a small lake to the left.

"And now, for the surprise," said Don. "Ta-da!" he announced, gesturing toward Belvedere Castle, which stood at the top of another hill, towering over the lake in front of them.

"Oh, my," Allison said, surveying the fortress in front of her. "I have never seen anything like it."

"Amazing, huh?" asked Don, pushing away some hair that had blown over his eyes.

"Absolutely amazing," answered Allison. "How did you discover it?"

"Well," Don explained, "I like to wander around on Saturdays after I finish my homework and my mother goes to work at the bar. One day, I was just meandering down this path and I discovered it. There it was. I couldn't believe it. Right here in New York City. A real, live castle!"

"Can you go inside?" asked Allison.

"Hmmm. I don't know about that," answered Don.

"Maybe we could find out," said Allison. "I wonder if it's haunted? Let's go see!" Allison proclaimed, as they turned to walk up the path to the big front door. "Wait'll I tell all my friends that I went to a castle in New York City!"

"I know, it's so exciting, isn't it?" asked Don.

"Wait a minute," said Allison, as she stopped in the middle of the path.

"What's the matter?" asked Don.

"They'll never believe me," said Allison, a little crestfallen.

"So?" asked Don. "Who cares what they think?"

"Yes, that's right!" proclaimed Allison. "Who cares?"

CHAPTER THIRTEEN

1957

Don was tired of being on the bus. He needed a break.

He wanted to do something different. He was ready to see the West, but not from the back of a Greyhound bus. Even though he had gotten the day off at Ivan's, his back was beginning to ache once more. Every time he got off and walked around, he noticed it took some time for him to walk normally because of the stiffness. He couldn't possibly get on another bus the way he felt.

They had just pulled into Missoula. He had to make his connection for Whitefish in an hour and even though it was only a few more hours he had to get out of it. He would come up with an explanation and change the ticket for tomorrow.

It was a crisp, clean day and the air smelled like it had just rained. Heading toward the ticket office, Don came up with an idea. "Excuse me," he said to the clerk, "I have to make the next bus to Whitefish, but I've had a change of plans. Is there a bus tomorrow that I can catch instead?"

"Tomorrow . . . Whitefish . . . let's see," the clerk said while he looked over his large schedule card. "Yes, tomorrow morning, there's a bus at 11:00 a.m."

"That's swell," Don answered. "Can I change my ticket, please?"

"Yes, you can," replied the clerk, "but there will be a one dollar service fee to make the change," the clerk said.

"Okay," said Don. "One dollar for a break from the bus will be well worth it," he said.

"Been on for a while, huh?" asked the clerk.

"Sure have," Don answered. "I got on in New York."

"New York?" the clerk responded. "My, my. We don't often get Greyhound passengers from New York."

"No, I don't guess you do," said Don.

"The ones for Glacier National Park usually fly these days. Well, what brings you to Montana from New York?" the clerk asked.

"Oh, family," Don mused. It sounded strange to say these words out West. He reached into his pocket and peeled off a dollar bill from a small roll. "Well, here's your dollar for the change."

"Thank you," the clerk said. "May I please see your original ticket?"

Don reached into his shirt pocket and pulled out the ticket, handing it to the clerk.

"Thank you," the clerk said, taking the ticket from him. Don watched him as he processed the change. He was a small man with clear Lucite glasses and a bald head. He wore a visor, as well as a vest with a pocket watch hanging from it and an armband that held his shirtsleeve in place. *He must have a very regular life,* Don pondered. *Predictable, but sure. I wonder what a life like that would be like?*

"Here you are," the clerk said. "One way to Whitefish, tomorrow at 11:00 a.m."

"Thank you very much," said Don, and walked away, feeling somehow lighter than before. Turning back, he approached the clerk once more. "I'm sorry, I forgot to ask. Where is the nearest Western Union office?"

"Go back out the entrance and make a right. It's two doors down," the clerk said.

"Thanks again," said Don.

"You're welcome, son," replied the clerk.

Making his way out the front door Don rehearsed the telegram he was going to write, which would be easier than talking on the telephone. He walked into the office and picked up a pad at the counter. He wrote to Velma and Sergei:

Arrived in Missoula. Slight delay. Everything okay. Will arrive tomorrow, 1:30 p.m. Don.

Don separated the finished telegram from the rest of the pad. A young woman with blond, shoulder-length hair and a navy blue dress approached him from behind the counter.

"Hello," Don said to her. "I'd like to send this to Whitefish, Montana."

"Whitefish, Montana," the young woman repeated, "and you have, let me see . . . ten words, that'll be $1.80." Don noticed how pretty she was.

He reached into his pocket for two dollars, which he peeled off his roll of bills. "There you are," he said, as he handed the woman the two singles.

"Two dollars," the woman took the money from Don. "And twenty cents is your change," she said, handing him two dimes. "Thank you very much." She smiled at Don.

"Thank you," said Don, and turned to leave the office. "Have a nice day!"

"You, too!" the young woman said, as she watched Don walk out the door.

As he stepped into the sun-filled street, Don suddenly felt at a loss. For the first time in days, he had nowhere he needed to immediately be. He continued to the right, walking with the other people in Missoula, looking at all the shops and thinking about what he would do next.

First, he had to find a place to stay for the night. Then he needed to shower and shave and get some lunch. After walking to the corner, Don realized he was getting tired. As much as he wanted to wander around town, he was also getting hungry. He turned around and decided to walk back to the bus station, where he could use the telephone booth.

When he got there, he sat down on the little seat and pulled up the telephone directory, opening it to look for hotels. "Missoula Hotel and Café," Don read with his finger over the name. "That sounds good." He got up, pulled on his backpack and headed back into the bus station lobby.

"Hello, it's me again," Don said to the ticket agent. "Can you tell me how I can get to the Missoula Hotel and Café?"

"Certainly," said the agent, smiling at Don. "You can get a taxi at the corner. It's about a ten-minute ride."

"Thanks," said Don. "You've been very helpful."

"Not at all," said the man. "Anytime."

At the corner, Don got into a waiting taxicab.

"Where to, sonny?" the driver asked.

"Missoula Hotel," Don answered.

"Alrighty then. Missoula Hotel it is," the driver said, pulling away from the curb.

Don settled back in his seat and looked out the window. He saw low buildings and shop fronts; people were walking on the sidewalks, just like they did in New York, but somehow, they looked different, not as formal. Some of the men wore cowboy hats. And beyond it all, rising from the town and into the sky, were massive, snow-covered mountains. Don was in awe. He had never seen a mountain, except in the movies.

After checking in at the hotel, Don showered and shaved. Looking at his reflection in the bathroom mirror he was stunned at how tired he still looked. In the full-length mirror on the closet door, Don examined his torso, to see if the rash that he assumed was caused by wearing the vest all that time had gone away. Sure enough, most of it was gone.

He dressed again and decided to go get some lunch. He was happy the café was in the hotel; he just wanted to have a sandwich and take a nap in a bed that wasn't a seat on a moving bus.

"You're from out of town," the young blond waitress said to Don. Her features were delicate, and she spoke in the kind of accent they had in the cowboy pictures.

"Yup," Don responded.

"Well, where are you traveling from?" she asked. Don noticed her smiling eyes.

"Chicago," Don said. He felt only a little badly about lying.

"Really?" the waitress responded. "Oh, I have always wanted to go to Chicago. I have a girlfriend, she went with her family. Well, they had the most amazing time. They took in a show, and they went to the Art Institute, and they had dinner out every night and, oh, she came home with the most darling dress from Marshall Field's. You've heard of Marshall Field's?"

"Uh-huh," Don said, picking up the check. He had finished his sandwich and coffee by now. "Well, I'll be heading out now."

"It's been nice talking to you," the waitress said, handing Don his change.

Back in the hotel room, Don pulled down the blinds and adjusted them so no light would come in while he slept. He lay down on the bed, letting his head collapse against the pillows. He stared at the ceiling, noticing a small crack in the paint. It reminded him of the crack in the ceiling in his bedroom in Yorkville, that looked like a tree branch, and how many years he had spent staring at it. He suddenly realized he would never see that crack again.

Don found himself at a crossroads. It was in a beautiful place with flat plains and mountains in the distance. He had stopped his car and was consulting a map, but it seemed to be of no help. "Excuse me," he asked another motorist stopping at the road. "Can you tell me how to get to . . . ?" The man just looked at him and drove away. "Ma'am?" he asked another driver who had slowed down, as well. "I'm lost and need to get to . . . can you help me?" The woman didn't even answer, just nodded her head from side to side and drove off into the distance. Finally, he saw a little boy, about eight, walking down the road. Don stopped the car and asked the boy for help. The boy looked quizzically at Don and pointed both arms in opposite directions.

He woke up, rubbing his eyes. At first, he wasn't sure where he was. Then it all became clear to him. He got up, went into the bathroom, and looked in the mirror. The bags under his eyes were a little less prominent and his eyes were not as pink. After combing his hair, he decided to go out and take a walk.

On the street Don felt better than he had in days and his back was starting to ache less. Even though he had been on the bus for what seemed like his whole life he felt like he was able to stretch and breathe the clean, cool air of Missoula. Walking down South Higgins, he took in the vista of the small city against the mountains and felt free. He stopped in front of Johnson Jewelry and admired the circular and rectangle-shaped watches that seemed to speak of an organized, sophisticated life. He had always had a Timex watch from Woolworth's, and he liked it, but it would be nice once day to graduate to something a little more adult-like.

He continued to walk and looked at the clothing in Furnishings by Herb. There were suits and ties. Don no longer owned a suit. The last one he wore was to a funeral of one of the bar patrons, Mr. Obricki. He came in every night and ordered two Pabst Blue Ribbons, one right after the other, then left to go home. Across the street, Don saw a bookstore. He had finished *A Death in the Family* and was ready to move on to something else. Crossing at the corner, he turned back and made his way towards McPherson & Stone, which displayed books in the window and had newspapers and stationery inside.

Don walked in and closed the door, whose bell tinkled when he pushed it shut. He looked around and began wandering the aisles, looking at various books. He picked up a copy of a play called *Look Back in Anger*. He read the back cover and several pages, then put it down. After wandering some more, he opened *The Complete Short Stories of Mark Twain* and began to read one. He had really enjoyed reading *The Adventures of Tom Saw-*

yer when he was in school. After putting it back in its place on the display table, Don wandered over to the postcard stand. He looked at the array for a few minutes, then selected one with a photograph of downtown Missoula with the mountains in the background: "Greetings from Missoula," it read. Don was about to purchase the card when he remembered he needed a book for the bus.

He walked back to the book aisle and found a table with a display sign that read *Recently Published*. Books such as *The Guns of Navarone; From Russia, with Love;* and *On the Road* were neatly stacked on it. Don picked up *The Guns of Navarone* and read the back cover, deciding to replace it because, although he was quite interested in stories about Word War II, he didn't feel like reading one on this trip. Don then looked at *From Russia, with Love*. He had read *Diamonds Are Forever* when it came out the previous year and really enjoyed it. Somehow, though, he was not in the mood for a thriller at this time.

Finally, Don's eye caught *On the Road,* a new work by the young Jack Kerouac.

A book about traveling across the country was exactly what Don was looking for. He read the front and back cover and opened the volume to the first page. While he read, he noted that the style was unlike anything Don had read before, very loose and flowing. As he continued to read, it seemed like the use of language was the exact opposite of the way Don was taught to write in school, using description and proper sentence structure. Kerouac's writing almost felt like a first draft. Fascinated, Don decided to purchase the book and took it, with the postcard, to the clerk at the front of the store by the window.

"*On the Road*," the man said. "You're a brave man."

"Really?" answered Don.

"Let me know what you think," said the clerk, as he wrapped the book in brown paper and fastened it with a piece of cellophane tape.

"I'll do that," Don answered. "Thanks so much."

With his package in hand, Don wandered to the back of the store, where there was a soda fountain. "Coca-Cola please," Don requested of the young man behind the counter.

"Sure," the man said.

"Say, do you have a pen I could borrow?" asked Don.

"Yup, here ya' go," said the waiter, handing him a pen from behind the counter.

Dear Ruth, Don was about to write on the postcard. Then he paused, looking up at the ceiling and taking a deep breath. *Dear Allison,* he wrote. *How are you? I'm on a trip. I'm on a bus out West. I miss you. Don.*

"Do you know where I could get an international stamp?" Don asked the waiter.

"Sure, we sell them up front," he said.

"Thanks," Don answered and finished drinking his soda. He left the shop with his book and walked down South Higgins, toward the Clark Fork River. At Madison Park, he found a bench that faced the water and sat down.

What a luxury, Don thought, *sitting still and not moving on a sunny day with a new book*. He unwrapped the package and turned the book over to read the back cover:

> "The most beautifully executed, the clearest and the most important utterance yet made by the generation Kerouac himself named years ago as "beat," and whose principal avatar he is."   —*The New York Times*

"Avatar . . . avatar," Don repeated out loud. *What does that mean?* he wondered. *And what is a "beat generation?"*

He opened the book to page one and started reading, as the massive Montana clouds sat suspended above him in the pale blue sky.

CHAPTER FOURTEEN

1953

"What are you getting?" Allison asked, as she leaned down to peer in the little glass window.

"Oh, I don't know," Don replied. "There are so many yummy choices."

"I have to say I love anything lemon," Allison responded, as she stared at the lemon chiffon pie.

"Me? I love a good apple anything," Don answered, as he reached into his pocket for some nickels. "I think I'll have the apple pie with vanilla sauce. "Let's go get our trays."

The automat had been Don's choice. He and Allison had been taking turns choosing fun spots to go to in the city that, hopefully, the other one had never been to.

"How did you find this place?" Allison asked, after deciding on the lemon meringue pie.

"Oh," Don answered, "I was riding by on the El, on the way to Uncle Sergei's, and I saw the red neon sign. Lots of people were going in at lunch time and I figured it must be good."

"Look at the coffee!" Allison proclaimed, as they both walked over to a wall where a customer placed their cup and saucer underneath a shiny animal head, fed a nickel into a slot, and turned a large chrome handle. The coffee spouted from the animal's mouth in a smooth dark stream landing in the diner's china cup.

"What *is* that?" Allison asked, as she strained to see the animal head close up.

"It's a dolphin!" Don said.

"Wow," Allison signed. "That's swell."

"Here," Don said, digging into his pocket. "I have several dollars. I think we have to get change. But I don't know where." He looked around.

"Whatcha do, see, is ya go over to the nickel thrower . . ." Don suddenly found himself speaking to a short, squat man in a worn suit and dusty Fedora.

"The nickel thrower?" Don asked.

"Yeah, the dame over there, in the little glass booth, see?" the man said pointing to the front of the commissary. "Ya give her your greenbacks and she gives you a fistful a nickels, see?"

"Gee, thanks, mister!" Don responded.

"Anytime, kid, anytime," the man said, as he turned and walked away. Don and Allison walked over to the kiosk, that resembled the information booth at Grand Central Terminal, only without the top on it.

"A dollar's worth of nickles, please." Don handed his bill to a lady with strawberry-blond hair and bright red lipstick.

"Here ya go, sonny. Have a blast," she told him, as she handed him a fistful of nickels.

"This is so much fun!" Allison said, as Don handed her half his change, which she placed in her coat pocket.

"I had a feeling you'd enjoy this," Don answered "knowing how much you like sweets. I've always wanted to come myself."

"Okay, who goes first?" Allison asked as they walked back to the wall of desserts. "You, and your apple, or me and my lemon?"

"You!" Don answered. "You go first!"

"Okay." Allison said. "Here goes." She reached into her pocket and took out two nickels, inserted them, one after the other, in the slot next to the lemon meringue pie, then turned the knob, and pulled the glass door up. "Wow," she proclaimed, as she took out the slice of pie, with sunshine yellow custard on the bottom and cloud white meringue on top.

"Look at that!" Don said. Allison had barely placed her treat on her tray when a new one appeared behind the glass door. "They sure don't waste time around here, huh?"

"No, I guess they don't," Allison responded. "Okay, your turn!" she said, as they proceeded to the multiple windows of heaping apple pie.

After Don removed his slice from its little compartment and they had each gotten a cup of dolphin-dispensed coffee they looked around to find two empty seats. "Over there!" Allison pointed, motioning to her left. As it turned out, the couple that was sitting at the table for four was leaving and the remaining seats were empty. "Gee, we get the table all to ourselves!" she proclaimed.

"Wow, I have a feeling *that* never happens," Don said.

As they settled into their seats Allison asked, "Now, mister, where are you taking me after this?" She had a twinkle in her eye.

"Oh, you'll see," Don answered, as he speared his fork into his slice of pie.

"Hmmm—a surprise, huh?" Allison said. "Well, won't you even give me a little hint?" she asked, as she scooped up a small bit of lemon meringue pie. "Oh, this is *good*. It's quite tart!"

"Well," said Don, putting his fork down on the plate, "a hint—okay, let me think." He looked up at the ceiling. "I think—I'm not positive—that you have never been to one."

"Oh," Allison mused, "so we've talked about this before, have we?" Now let me see. Is it indoors or outdoors?" she asked before taking another bite of pie.

"No, no, no. You already got your hint! You only get one," Don countered, as he picked up his fork once more.

"Oh, all right," Allison said. "Say, how's your apple pie?"

"It's good!' Don replied. "It's not too sweet. I hate when pie has too much sugar." He took a bite then looked at his watch. "Well, we oughta finish up and get going."

"Oh, I get it! We're on a schedule," Allison smiled at him.

"Yes, we are," Don answered, returning the smile.

When they had taken their last bites, they put their plates back on the tray and walked over to the drop-off station, where a conveyor belt whisked their plates and cups away. "They sure are efficient around here," Allison commented, as she watched their dishes disappear into a square at the end of the shiny steel wall. "Now, where to, sir?" Allison asked, as she slipped her arm into Don's, and they headed for the door.

"That's for me to know and you to find out," Don winked at her, as they tucked themselves into the revolving door.

On 42nd Street, Don and Allison turned right and walked to the corner to catch the El. As they climbed the stairs, Allison said, "So, we have to take the train there. Okay, now let me guess. Uptown or downtown?"

On the uptown platform, Don started giggling while they waited for the train.

"What's so funny?" Allison asked.

"Oh, nothing," Don said. "It's just that you don't see a man in a cowboy hat in New York that often."

"A *cowboy* hat!" Allison proclaimed.

"Yeah, a cowboy hat," Don responded, pointing

to a man walking away from them, wearing a white cowboy hat in a sea of grey Fedoras.

"I wonder where he's from," Allison mused, staring at the rapidly disappearing hat.

"Me, too," Don chuckled.

"Now what's so funny?" Allison prodded.

"Oh, nothing," Don responded.

The train was already crowded when they got on and there were no seats to be found. "Do you ever wonder where all these people are going?" Allison asked.

"I do," Don answered, as they found two straps to hang on to. "I've often wondered that myself."

The train suddenly lurched and Don and Allison were thrown together momentarily. "Well, hello there!" Don said. "Fancy meeting you here."

"Indeed," Allison answered. "Do you come here often?"

"Here's our stop!" Don announced, as they pulled into the 84th Street station.

"84th Street!" Allison protested. "But that's *our* stop. Are we going home?"

"No, silly, we aren't going home." Don replied. "We're going somewhere *near* home." When they got to the bottom of the stairs, Don steered them north on Third Avenue, then right on 86th Street.

"Don, *where* are we going?" Allison asked, as they crossed Second Avenue.

"Ta-da!" Don announced, when they got to the 86th Street Grande. "We're here!"

"Oh! We're going to the movies!" Allison said

as she looked up at the marquee. "*Shane*. What's it about?"

"It's a Western. I've been waiting for ages for this one to come out!" Don approached the clerk in the booth. "Two tickets, please,"

"I'm so excited," Allison said. "I've never seen a Western before."

"That's what I thought," said Don. He had seen the advertisements for it and was hoping Allison would join him. He liked the idea that it took place in the West but that there was also a little boy in the story. He wanted to know what happened to him.

"I love Westerns. *Ramrod, Red River, Yellow Sky . . .*" Don continued.

"Wow, you've seen a lot of them," Allison commented.

"I guess I have," Don replied. "Would you like some popcorn?" he asked Allison, as they approached the concession stand.

"Sure," said Allison. "I love popcorn!"

The movie theatre was large and had overstuffed red velvet seats and an ornate ceiling that was painted gold. "Is this okay?" Don asked Allison, pointing to a row of seats in the middle of the theatre.

"Perfect," Allison said, as they started making their way between the seats.

As they settled themselves in Don put the popcorn and Coca-Cola on the floor so that he could take Allison's jacket and place it on the seat beside him.

"This is so much fun," Allison said as she started

munching on some popcorn. "I don't go to the movies very often."

"Me neither," said Don.

"I didn't know you like Westerns," said Allison, taking a handful of popcorn from the bag.

"I do," said Don, taking a sip of Coca-Cola. "They really take me out of this city. I can't believe people actually live in places like that."

"I know," said Allison, taking the Coca-Cola from Don. "It's funny to think that while we're here, dealing with cars and trucks and subways and noise, there are people surrounded by trees and grass and mountains and all that sky."

"Right?" asked Don, helping himself to the popcorn. "What do they do all day?"

"Oh, I suppose they go to school like we do," said Allison, "and their parents are farmers or maybe they're miners. There must be doctors and nurses. It's probably not all that different from where we are except that the surroundings are different. And I suppose there just aren't as many people as there are in a big city like New York."

"Yeah, I guess you're right about that," said Don. "But it sure is prettier."

The previews started and Don suddenly felt happy. He couldn't remember the last time he had felt that way. No, he was wrong. He *could* remember. It was the last time he was with Allison. Whenever he was with her, he seemed to forget about everything else and feel a kind of calm that he felt with no one else.

When the film started, and the lights went off completely, Allison slipped her hand inside Don's. He relaxed and leaned back into his seat. He was so grateful for Allison. Her companionship had provided something that had been missing from his life: someone to talk to, laugh with, and share experiences, like going to the movies, or having ice cream, and going to Central Park together.

Allison leaned over and put her head on Don's shoulder. They sat like this for several moments. Then he shifted and placed his left arm behind her and started to run his fingers through her dark hair, which was loose this evening. Sometimes she wore her hair in braids, but mostly she wore it pulled back into a ponytail.

They sat like this for a while and then Allison lifted her head off of Don's shoulder. He thought she was going to move away. Instead, she leaned in towards him and kissed him on the cheek. He turned to her and she touched her lips to his. Don was completely taken aback and delighted at the same time. They kissed for much of the film. When it ended, they decided to stay for the next screening, so they could see what they had missed the first time around.

CHAPTER FIFTEEN

1955

Dark, inky clouds expanded in the sky as they walked to Regis High School. Don was wearing his gown and he carried his cap in a paper shopping bag. He liked the way the gown billowed in the wind as he walked.

"I hope it no rain until we get to ceremony," Velma said, thinking about the gown that she had spent so much time pressing, getting wrinkled in the rain.

"Yes," Sergei responded, looking up at the sky over 84th Street. "Hopefully, it will hold off until we are inside."

Don was excited about his high school graduation. Things were going really well and there was a lot to celebrate. He'd had a good senior year and received excellent grades. There were some new friends he had made at school—Henry and George—and when he wasn't working at the bar, Don found time after homework to socialize with them. He and Allison continued to see each other, and they were even considering a future together. At the same time, though, Don could not believe this period of his childhood was over. He had been in school for as long as he could remember. Every year was similar to the previous year, only Don and his friends got bigger, and school got harder.

For Don, the biggest transition was to Regis High School.

It had all started with Don, entering the bar one day, and asking Velma if he could go to a Catholic high school in the neighborhood.

"What?" Velma asked, incredulous. "What is this Regis High School?"

"It's a Catholic school," Don responded. "Up on Park Avenue and 84th."

"Park Avenue?!" Velma was astounded. "Who you think you are?" She returned to sweeping the floor. "What you talking about—Park Avenue!"

"No, Ma, it's not like that," Don replied. "Yes, it's on Park Avenue, but it's a really good school and all the boys are not rich. In fact, a lot of them are on scholarship."

"Scholarship?" Velma asked. "What is this scholarship?"

"It's when the school helps you pay for your education," Don replied, "because your grades are so good. It's for students like me who take school really seriously. Mr. Jones, our principal, told me I was a candidate, because I am such a strong student, and that I should consider applying. Some other boys from my school are also applying."

"So, they pay for everything?" Velma asked.

"Well, I don't know about everything . . ." Don answered. "I have to find out. The point is, this would be an opportunity for me to have a better education than the one I have now. I'm sick and tired of defending the fact that I like learning."

"Well, on this you have point. Learning is everything." Velma paused, leaning the broom against the counter. She turned to Don. "You talk to Sergei. He must look into this."

To his surprise, Sergei thought Regis was a wonderful opportunity for Don.

"I have been concerned for you and your education," he stated, when Don brought up the subject of the scholarship. "I don't like what I've been hearing about the local high school," he said. "A lot of hooligans there."

"Yes," Don replied. "That's what I was worried about, too. I think I'll concentrate better at a school where there are so many good students." Don was thrilled Sergei understood. They didn't always see eye to eye on things, and he was excited that Sergei was supportive of his attending Regis. Velma had finally capitulated, saying that she would agree, if Don passed the scholarship exam and Sergei wanted to pay for the remainder of his education. Sergei's position was that Don's excellent grades made him a candidate for a scholarship and that "when life presents such an opportunity one does not pass it up."

Don studied as hard as he could, and the day

finally came for him to take the exam. He found it quite challenging and, when it was over, went home quite dejected.

"Don," Sergei asked, when he saw him at the bar that evening. "How did you do on the entrance exam?"

"Oh," Don replied as he polished a beer glass, "I don't think I did very well. It was much harder than I expected."

"Yes, I assumed it would be a difficult exam," Sergei replied. "But Don, you haven't gotten your results back. You don't *know* you didn't pass it. You just know that it was a strenuous test. I have taken many difficult exams in my life, and you really don't know the results until the results are revealed."

Don thought for a minute before he replied. "I guess that's true," Don answered, as he replaced the glass under the bar. Sometimes Sergei surprised Don by saying things that made even the most trying situations more bearable.

When the letter arrived, a month later, Don hesitated before opening it. He was convinced he had failed the test and that he was holding a rejection letter in his hand. Then he remembered Sergei's words and realized that he had no idea what the letter would say. To his utter surprise, he was accepted.

At first, it was hard saying goodbye to his friends from public school. Don suddenly felt there was a difference between them—he was going to the Park Avenue school and his buddies, whom he had known since childhood, were going to the local Board of Education high school. It felt awkward and made for some uncomfortable conversations in the school yard. This wasn't something Don was prepared for. Although Don was looking forward to going to Regis, it was hard to picture what the future would look like.

As it turned out, the first semester was rough—the lessons were much harder than Don had anticipated, and there were many hours of homework every night. Public school certainly hadn't prepared him for this. He got to know some new boys, however, in addition to a few who had also come from the neighborhood, and by the time the Christmas holiday came around, Don had started to settle in. In the spring, he joined the softball team, which he really enjoyed because the boys got to play in Central Park. In the fall of his sophomore year, Don felt like he belonged at Regis.

He was walking a few feet ahead of Velma and Sergei, and when he got to the corner of 84th Street and Park Avenue he waited for the traffic light to change. Don looked up at the sky and was thrilled the rain had held off, after all.

Behind him, Don could hear Velma and Sergei approaching and their conversation.

"No!" Velma was proclaiming to Sergei. She was on the verge of tears. "This must not happen!"

"Velma, please," Sergei pleaded. "It might not be so bad for the boy."

"But this is just it," she replied. "He is a boy. He not ready for the military."

They were nearing the corner. "But we mustn't talk about this now," Sergei proclaimed. "First, we celebrate!"

As he listened to them, Don wondered why his special evening had to be colored by talk of the draft.

As they crossed the street, and entered through the side entrance on 84th Street, Don thought about graduation and how proud he was of himself for making it this far. He couldn't believe it was happening to him. He saw the older kids go through this right of passage ahead of him, but it seemed like something that only happened to other students, that he would never be a part of this ceremony himself. And then there were many boys in the neighborhood who dropped out of high school and never graduated at all.

In the large auditorium where the ceremony was to be held, Don left Velma and Sergei at the seats that were assigned to families. He then made his way to the green room off the stage so that he could adjust his cap and make sure the tassels were properly positioned. There was excitement in the air and the boys were nervously talking amongst themselves. "Hey, Don!" George poked him, "I've got Mike and Ikes!" he proclaimed, pulling out the small box of candy from his jacket pocket. "It's gonna be a long one!" he groaned.

"Excellent!" Don agreed, smiling at George, who was always planning ahead.

The boys all gathered in their scarlet, silver, and white gowns, while Dean Halsey, the Regis headmaster, inspected their caps, making sure they fit correctly on their heads and that their tassels were on the right side. Finally, Don got into his place near the end of the line, still feeling like he was watching someone else take part in this event, not himself. Dean Halsey asked the boys for complete silence, and they stood there, simply waiting, until they were given the command to climb the small flight of stairs to the stage.

The boys walked to the folding seats in single file, just as they had rehearsed for days before. The school band was playing "Pomp and Circumstance", and the audience members clapped as the boys found their places, but, as he sat down, all Don could think of was that he was in the back row and maybe Velma and Sergei couldn't see him. The stage lights were so bright that he couldn't make anyone out in the audience.

Finally, the music ended as the last boy, Harry Williams, sat down next to Don. Dean Halsey began speaking, welcoming family and friends, and telling them how proud he was of the class of '55. He went on to list the multiple sports awards the school had won, before mentioning the ever increasing amount of college acceptances they had gotten that year. Finally, he put forth the impressive university list, which included such prestigious institutions as West Point and the U.S. Naval Academy at Annapolis.

"Daniel Vasiliev!" Dean Halsey called and Don slowly stood up, feeling very important. He walked to the podium and accepted his diploma, shaking the dean's hand. There was lots of clapping and cheering from the audience and Don knew that Velma and Sergei were part of this. He just wished he could see their jubilant faces.

After the ceremony there was a big party for the graduating class and families in the school gym. Don looked around until he found Velma and Sergei.

"My boy, my Dontchik!" Velma squeezed him. "How you get to be so big!"

"Ma!" Don chastised her. "Stop!" But he was smiling all the while. Indeed, he was big, almost a head taller than Velma, and even a few inches taller than Sergei.

"Boys, gather 'round for a photo!" Mr. Jones, Henry's father commanded. Don, Henry, and George stood next to each other, their faces beaming. "Say cheese!" Henry's father yelled out, as he took the picture. "Now, let's get the families in," he continued. As Velma and Sergei walked up to take part in the photo Don noticed, for the first time that evening, that Velma was wearing a new dress for the occasion. She had actually gone out and bought herself a new outfit. This made Don feel even more special. Velma rarely went out or did anything for herself.

"Don, we are so proud of you," Sergei proclaimed as he gave Don a big hug.

Several other families were congregating around the refreshments table and a conversation had started between Sergei and Mr. Tomlinson, the father of one of the other graduates, as they both reached for glasses at the punch bowl. Many of the boys grabbed bottles of soda pop that lined the table. After the initial small talk, Mr. Tomlinson asked Sergei about the Selective Service officer who had come to the school last month.

"I was surprised," he said, "when Joe Jr. came home. "I didn't think he would be excited about the draft. Turns out, he likes the idea. He came home and told us everything the representative said in his presentation. Ya never know with these kids today."

"Yes," Sergei replied. "Don told us about it, as well, and I feel that this is a good opportunity for him. He will have a different experience. It will make him a man."

"That's what these kids need," Mr. Tomlinson continued. "They need to become good citizens and learn how to defend their country. They need to work, not sit around and cause trouble on the streets."

"I agree. This hooligan activity we've been hearing about in the neighborhood," said Sergei. "And the gang fighting. All very disturbing."

"I don't know what's happening to the youth of today," Mr. Tomlinson was saying. "Why when I was a kid, we were afraid of our parents because they threatened us if we did not behave. We were beaten with belts. I'm sure you were, as well. If we did not behave, we knew what was coming. These children? They have no fear."

"Yes, this is true," Sergei responded.

"Also," Mr. Tomlinson went on, "we worked as soon as we could. There were always odd jobs available for us kids. We sold papers, and ran errands for the neighbors, anything to get out of the house and make some pocket money. This made us feel like we were adults. It gave us responsibility. These kids today, I see them laying about on the stoops and I think to myself that no good will come of this."

"Yes," Sergei continued. "It's very important for them to work from a young age. Our Don, he always had what you call the odd jobs in the neighborhood, from the time he was a boy. And, of course, he also helped out at the bar. So, he has grown up working."

"That's good! That's the way it should be," Mr. Tomlinson agreed. "Unfortunately, my wife is not as excited as Joe Jr. is. She's worried he'll get called up."

"Yes, Velma has similar concerns," said Sergei. "She is not happy about it at all. But Don? Interestingly, he's not that concerned. He doesn't think he'll get called up. Isn't that right, Don?" Sergei asked as Don, Henry and George approached them.

"It is. I think it won't happen," Don responded.

"Well, you might be right," Mr. Tomlinson said. "There's talk that they have too many young men registered already. They can't possibly use all of them. Perhaps you've heard this rumor."

"Ah, I see," Sergei responded. "That would make sense. I shall tell Velma this. Hopefully, it will make her feel better."

"Yes, the women see this thing differently than us men do," Mr. Tomlinson said.

"Yes, they do," said Sergei, as he began to look around the gym for Don and Velma. "Well . . . it was a pleasure speaking with you," he said, turning back to Mr. Tomlinson. Congratulations to Joe, Jr. and to your family." Sergei held out his hand.

"Yes, and to you as well," responded Mr. Tomlinson, shaking Sergei's hand.

After the refreshments ran out and the graduates and their families started to leave the building, Sergei located Velma, who was speaking with some of the other mothers.

"Yes, I hope that they do have too many boys registered already," Henry's mother, Mrs. Jones, was saying.

"Ach, I pray to God that this is true," Velma responded. "They just boys—children—they not ready to leave home and go into military."

"I couldn't agree more," Mrs. Jones said.

"Well, if you can," Mrs. Sunderson said to Velma as she saw Sergei approaching "we would love to have your help for the church Fourth of July picnic."

"Yes, I will help," Velma responded. "I call you."

"Thank you, Velma," Mrs. Sunderson said. "We look forward to seeing you."

"Thank you," said Velma. "Good night."

"Good night, and congratulations," Sergei said, as he took Velma by the arm, leading her to the exit with the other families.

It was dark when they exited the building, and the streets were shimmering. The rain had started, leaving puddles that mirrored the streetlights, as Don, Velma and Sergei walked home.

"Here," Sergei said to Velma, "I have one umbrella. "Don, you don't have one?"

"No, I'll be okay," Don replied. "I like walking in the rain." He watched the droplets slowly cover his gown.

"As you wish," Sergei replied.

"Dontchik, you catch cold in rain," Velma chastised.

"Ma!" Don almost yelled. "I just graduated high school! For cryin' out loud!" He walked ahead of them as far as he could.

"Velma, it is all right," Sergei said. "The boy is a man now." Then, he continued, "I was just speaking with Mr. Tomlinson, Joe Jr's father, at the refreshment table. I know how upset you are about Selective Service. His wife is, too. But one thing he said may give you hope."

"What is this?" Velma asked.

"Well," Sergei continued. "It seems they may have too many young men for Selective Service. Now, I am not sure about this. It may just be a rumor. But this is certainly something we should look into, don't you think?"

"Yes!" Velma pleaded. "Yes, we *must* look into this."

As they talked, Don distracted himself with the pink neon Billy's Bar and Grill sign reflected on the wet sidewalk and the raindrops that bounced on the surface.

CHAPTER SIXTEEN

1957

On the bus to Whitefish, Don felt better. It was only going to be a few hours now and he felt like a new human being, physically. Having had a real night's sleep and a shower and shave had given him a fresh start. He had really enjoyed walking around Missoula and getting to know the town a little. He even thought he could see himself living in a place like this one day.

As rested as he felt, there was a slight pain in the pit of his stomach. He had to begin preparing for the drama ahead in his mind. *I'm not staying* he would say. *I've transported your money and now it's time for me to move on. You'll have to find someone else to help you.* There would be a scene. He knew that. He was simply going to have to face it. It wasn't going to be easy.

Don looked out the window and watched the road, mountains and sky pass him by. When he and Allison had gone to see *Shane,* he was amazed at the expanding vistas. Sometime he would have to come back to Wyoming and see the Grand Tetons, where *Shane* took place. He and Allison had had that conversation about growing up in the West. Now he was here, even though he was only a visitor, and he could not get over how different it was from New York. He wondered what it must be like to grow up in a place like this. He had a different accent and did not dress the same way as the folks he saw in the towns he visited.

Kids must have grown up very differently out West. Don's childhood wasn't bad. It just seemed different from the way even his own friends grew up. He could tell because when he remembered Yorkville, it was always from the point of view of the bar and not from the amount of time he spent playing on the street. Don always felt that he was watching his friends play stickball or driving their soap box cars outside while he worked for Velma inside. He didn't want to be working all the time or going to school. He wanted more time to be a kid like all the others in the neighborhood.

As the bus drove by tall pine trees set against a backdrop of enormous mountains, Don wondered if his friends ever saw scary things happen in their families. One afternoon, when Don was around thirteen, he was walking home from school, and he had to stop by the bar. On most days, Velma asked him to go home first, drop off his books and get himself a snack before he headed over to the bar to help her out. This day was different, though, because she needed him to run an errand for her.

"Dontchik, you come to bar after school," Velma instructed. "I need you to do something for me. I have sandwich for you at bar to eat when you come."

He gave the knock that he always gave before the bar opened at 5:30 p.m. so that Velma knew it was him: tap-tap, pause, then tap-tap-tap. A few minutes later, Velma unlocked and opened the door. "Ah, Dontchik, you here. Good." She let him in and closed and locked the door again. "You come with me. I give you something." Don followed Velma to the back room. "You take this to hardware store," she said, handing Don a hinge. "I need new one like this to fix back door. Mr. Smolnecki will fix when you get back. He ask me to get because he is at doctor this afternoon."

"Okay, Ma," Don said. "I'm hungry. Can I have that sandwich?"

"Yes, of course. Here," Velma said, handing him a brown paper bag she retrieved from the cooler under the bar.

As he ate his ham and cheese sandwich at Velma's desk, Don listened to the sounds from the back window, which faced a small yard with a chain link fence and the garden he and Velma had planted. It was doing nicely, he noticed. There were tomatoes and small lettuces coming up, as well as sweet william and cosmos flowers. Velma's was the only garden as far as he could see. All the other back yards were waist high in weeds. "Such a shame," Velma would say, looking across the fence. "They should plant garden."

From upstairs he heard the sounds of the neighbors. *That couple is always yelling at each other,* Don thought. When he had finished the sandwich, Don rolled up the wax paper and bag, threw them away in the wastepaper basket by the side of Velma's desk, stood up, and headed for the front door. "Okay, Ma. I'll go now," Don called out.

"Yes, Dontchik. Thank you," Velma replied as she polished a glass behind the bar.

Don unlocked the door and headed out, turning right on 84th Street. For some reason, he just happened to look across the street, where he saw a young man, probably in his late twenties, dressed in a dark hat and a light blue suit, leaning against a fence. *That's funny,* thought Don. *He's so slickly dressed. He kinda looks out of place on this block.* Don continued to walk towards Second Avenue and waited at the crosswalk. When he got to the other side of the street, Don walked at a good pace but got the strange sense that he was not alone. He walked a bit faster, then noticed that his heart rate was increasing. He decided to stop in front of the barber shop in the middle of the block and go in to say hello.

"Don, hello! Long time no see, my boy," said the barber, looking up from the customer he was attending to.

"Hey, Mr. Anthony. Yeah, I need to come in but not today. I—" Don leaned out the window to see if he could get a look at the man outside.

"Something wrong, Don?" asked Mr. Anthony.

"I, uh . . . I'm not sure . . . I think someone might be following me."

"What?" Mr. Anthony asked, putting down his scissors. "Why?" asked.

"I don't know. I just have this funny feeling," Don answered.

"Let me take a look," said Mr. Anthony and he walked over to lean out the window. "I don't see anyone . . ." he said.

"Well okay, thanks, Mr. Anthony," said Don, looking out the window one more time.

"Listen, if you're in any kind of trouble, Don, you come right back, ya hear?" Mr. Anthony said.

"Thanks, Mr. Anthony," Don replied, as he walked out the door.

"You come back for that haircut sometime soon, Don!" called Mr. Anthony.

"Yeah . . . sure," said Don, as he slowly closed the door, making sure the bell didn't ring.

Trying to turn slightly to the left to see if the man was still there, Don turned around and continued to walk up 84th Street. Don wondered whether he was imagining things. Didn't he just see the man hiding in the entrance down the street?

At Third Avenue, Don crossed to the west side of the street and walked to Ackerman Hardware, in the middle of the block. A bell jingled over the door when he entered.

"What can I help you with, young man?" asked a stocky clerk with sandy brown hair.

"I need a hinge, please. One just like this," he

said, as he pulled out the hinge Velma had given him from his jacket pocket.

"Sure, just a minute," said the clerk, as he examined the hinge, then walked to the back of the store.

Don waited, looking around at the paint cans, pieces of lumber, and small light fixtures hanging from the ceiling. He shifted from one foot to the other because he loved the way the long wooden floorboards creaked under him.

"Here ya go," said the clerk, handing him a shiny new hinge just like the one he already had, and accompanying screws. "Step over to the register, please."

"Thank you," said Don, after the clerk had rung him up. Don exited the store and looked from left to right to see if the man was anywhere to be seen. Crossing Third Avenue and walking back down 84th Street, Don told himself that he had been imagining he was being followed. He wasn't sure what had prompted him to think anyone would want to trail him. But when he got back to the entrance of the bar, the man was right behind him.

"What do you want?" Don decided he had to be brave. He turned and faced the man directly.

"Relax, sonny, I just want to ask your mother some questions," the man said, grinning.

"What kind of questions?" Don asked. He could feel his heart rate escalating.

"Just some adult questions—nothing you need to concern yourself with. Let's go in and see her, shall we?" the man asked Don.

"She's not in right now," Don said.

"Sure, she is. Don't try to pull that one on me. I saw her let you out and I don't think she's gone anywhere since then," the man said.

Don paused, wondering whether he could stall for time. Reluctantly, realizing he was trapped, he gave the secret knock on the door. After a minute, Velma came to the front window and looked over the low curtain rod at Don. She then noticed the man standing next to him.

After the door slowly opened, Don said, "Ma, I'm sorry. He followed me here."

"He follow you?" Velma asked, with a concerned look on her face.

"Yes," Don said, looking down.

"Sure, I followed him. He took me on a little tour of the neighborhood," the man said.

"What you want?" Velma asked the man.

"Why don't you and me have a little conversation inside?" the man stated, ushering them both into the bar.

Seeing she had no choice, Velma closed the door after them, careful not to lock it.

"Nice little place you got here," the man said, looking around. "Seems like you take in a good amount considering you've just got a neighborhood bar."

Velma and Don stared at him. "You go to back room," Velma said, turning to Don.

"No, Ma, I'm staying right here," he said, moving closer to her side.

"There's no reason for him to go and hide. We're just having a friendly conversation, Miss Velma." He pushed the brim of his hat up a little off his head. "Now, I have a friend," the man said, "he's kind of a business associate, you could say, who's interested in what you do here."

"What I 'do?'" Velma asked. "I run bar."

"Oh, I think we all know you don't just run a bar," the man said.

"I know nothing what you talk about," Velma said. "I think you go now," Velma walked behind the bar and picked up a beer bottle.

"Now, take it easy," the man said. "All I said was we were just having a talk. No need to get upset."

"I no upset," said Velma. "You go. You get out of my place." Slowly, she started walking out from behind the bar, with the beer bottle still in her hand, but slightly higher than it was before. "You. Get. Out." By this time, Velma was standing in front of the man.

"Okay, Velma," he said, turning to the door. "You have it your way. Maybe my friend and I will pay you a visit some other time." He opened the door and walked out. "See ya!" he saluted her as he turned to the right and headed up 84th Street.

Velma locked the door and watched to make sure he was gone. Then she put the beer bottle down on the bar. She went behind the bar and took out a shot glass and a bottle of Stolichnaya. She held up the shot glass for Don to see. "You want?" she asked Don.

"No, Ma," Don answered. "What was that all about? What did that man want?"

"I don't know," Velma said. "He ..." she stopped short.

"What?" asked Don. "He what?"

"I never see him. Never before. I call Sergei," she said, putting down her shot glass on the bar, and going to the telephone booth in the back of the bar.

Don overheard her. "Sergei, you must come ... a man, a man I never see before, he came to the bar ... he said something about 'a friend' ... he's interested in what I do ... he says maybe they'll come to visit me together ... when? ... yes ... please ... goodbye." Velma hung up the telephone. "He come now," she said to Don, staring at the wall.

Don suddenly felt weak. He realized he had been standing the whole time the man was in the bar. He went behind the bar and poured himself a glass of water. Then he pulled an upside-down chair from the top of one of the tables along the wall and sat down. Dozens of thoughts were swirling around his brain all at the same time. Who was that man? What did he want? Why was he grilling Velma? What did he know about the bar?

He racked his brain to figure out who the man was. He looked neither familiar nor local. He certainly wasn't a patron of the bar. But he knew all about it. Which meant only one thing: the bar was being watched. But by whom? And why?

Don's head ached. He got up and went behind

the bar to refill his water glass. Now it was Velma's turn to sit down. She poured herself another shot while Don drank his water and they both stared into space.

CHAPTER SEVENTEEN

1955

The sound of clanging greeted Don every afternoon when he came home from school. They were demolishing the Third Avenue El.

Before, there was the sound of the train going by. Also, of loud, squalling birds. Pigeons would make their nest underneath the elevated tracks. Don never understood this until one day, when he stood and listened to the birds, an older man who was also watching them offered an explanation.

"They build 'em there," the man said, "because it's high in the sky and they're safe from predators. Also, it's dark and that's the way they like it."

"Gee, I never realized that," Don responded. "I never did understand why they'd want to build their nests up there."

"Yup," the man continued. "Dark, high, and safe," he said as he walked away.

Now that they were dismantling the El, there was the incessant banging of the hammers as the men took apart the system, piece by piece. Whereas

Don would formerly sit and watch the trains go by, as well as listen to the birds, now he sat and saw the men take the train away. He wondered where the birds were going to go.

At eighteen, Don had a lot of memories. There was the time he rode alone to Chatham Square and got soaked in a rainstorm in Chinatown. The day he and Allison rode to 42nd Street, had dessert at the automat and went to see *Shane*. They also went to the 42nd Street library together. They stayed for hours, looking at the books and the funny way they were brought to the patrons in something called "pneumatic tubes". They were immensely entertained by the numbers that came up on the board when the books arrived from the stacks in the basement.

There was the morning that Don rode the train to Sergei's. It had started snowing. He stood on the platform and watched the snowflakes blow from side to side, as if they could not decide what direction they were headed in. It was an early November snow and Don realized, as he stood on the platform, that it was time for him to get a new winter jacket. His hands were sticking out from the sleeves of the one he was wearing. The cuffs were too short, and they were fraying at the edges. He laughed to himself; when Velma bought him the jacket it was two sizes too big. He would have to ask her about getting a new one at Ar-Bee's. Don checked his inside pocket to make sure he had the envelope that Velma had given him for Sergei. He would be in big trouble if he lost it.

"Here is envelope," Velma had said. "You take to Sergei."

"Well, okay Ma. What's in it?" Don asked.

"You no worry 'what's in it'. You just take to him." Velma replied.

"Sure, Ma," said Don. There was no point in asking Velma anything after she said the words 'You no worry.' Don had learned that a long time ago.

As he stepped onto the train, he had a passing thought that Velma wasn't well. He'd had these feelings before and kept telling himself that he was imagining things, but this time the thoughts kept coming back on a regular basis. There had been a call to the bar from a doctor. When they asked for Velma and Don told the secretary that she was not there, the lady would not leave a detailed message. She just told Don to "have your mother call the doctor back." Then there was the time Velma asked Don to go to the drug store for her but wouldn't tell him what the prescription was for. Another day, Velma asked Don to tend bar for her. He had just come home from school and was surprised to find Velma at home. Usually, she would be at the bar by now.

"Dontchik," Velma said, as he opened the door. "I no well. You need to help me at bar tonight."

"What?" asked Don. "What's wrong, Ma?"

"I have cold," she said and started coughing fitfully.

Don had noticed the cough several days earlier but became concerned when Velma said she couldn't work. She had never missed a day of work for as long as he could remember.

"Okay," said Don. "But have you called the doctor?"

"Ach, doctors, what do they know?" replied Velma. "I have medicine. I know what to do," as she sipped her tea, which Don assumed had been laced with vodka or whiskey.

"Ma, you need to call the doctor," Don implored.

"Dontchik, you go and work at bar. I be okay," said Velma.

Don went into his room and dropped off his bag. "I'll make myself a sandwich," he said as he came back into the kitchen and opened the icebox.

"You good boy," said Velma. "Thank you."

"Yeah, sure," said Don, defeated. *Why does she never listen to me?* he wondered.

When he finished eating his sandwich, Don grabbed his coat and headed out the door. Then he turned around and went back in. "Ma, are you going to be okay?" he asked.

"Yes, Dontchik, I be okay," Velma responded, coughing into her handkerchief.

Don closed and locked the door as Velma continued to cough.

As he walked down 82nd Street, to Second Avenue, his normal route to the bar, Don had a frightening thought. What would he do if Velma got really sick? Even worse, what if she died? He could not imagine life without her.

Turning the key in the lock on the bar door,

Don instinctively looked around both ways on 84th Street to see if anyone was watching him but no one seemed to be in sight. Ever since the incident with the man in the blue suit, Don had become wary of anyone on the street that didn't look like they belonged in the neighborhood. He closed and locked the door and started taking down the chairs from the tables. In the light coming in from the street, he noticed the bar looked a bit dusty. Velma must've forgotten to wipe it down since she had not been feeling well. *Why hasn't she called the doctor*, Don wondered. *What is she not telling me?*

Don got a clean rag from under the bar and started wiping down all the surfaces that looked dusty. Then he looked at the glasses on the lower shelf and got another rag to polish them. *Maybe I should call the doctor*, he thought. He looked at the liquor bottles and found that they were all full enough. Then he opened the icebox to check the beer stock. It was a little low. Velma probably hadn't been feeling well enough to replenish it the night before. Going to the back room, Don found a key on a ring hanging from a hook on the wall. He walked to the front door, unlocked it, went out to the street, and placed the key inside the lock attached to the double metal basement doors in the sidewalk. Pulling both heavy doors open, he walked down the cement stairs and pulled the string attached to the light bulb in the ceiling. On one of the shelves along the wall he found a box of Pabst Blue Ribbon and hauled it down, making his way back up the stairs with the box on his shoulder. As he lay the box down on the sidewalk and went back down the stairs to turn off the light, he heard a knock at the bar door.

"Velma," a man's voice was calling. "Velma, you there?"

Don turned off the light and walked up the stairs, pulling the metal doors down and locking them.

"Oh, hello, Mr. Semyonov," Don said to one of the neighborhood regulars. "Bar's not open yet."

"Ah, Don! Velma, she is here?" Mr. Semyonov asked.

"No, she's not coming in tonight. She's not feeling well," said Don.

"What is wrong?" asked Mr. Semyonov.

"I don't know. I think she has a bad cold," said Don.

"I see," said Mr. Semyonov. "Well, you tell to her I need talk to her soon," and he turned away. "She maybe needs something?" He turned back.

"Thanks—I think she's okay," said Don. "I'll let you know if we need anything," he continued as he opened the door to the bar.

He put down the box and locked the door, then proceeded to carry the box to the bar so that he could restock the icebox, making sure he shuffled the bottles so that the warm ones that he had just unloaded from the box were at the back and the cold ones were at the front. *What if she isn't okay?* Don asked himself. *What would I do?* Dark and frightening thoughts started swirling around in Don's head and he almost dropped a bottle on the floor because he was so lost in them. *Stop,* he told himself. *Dontchik, you must pay attention,* Velma would have said. He listened to her, in his head, then told himself she is going to be okay.

Don looked at his watch and saw that it was 5:20. He would have to open the bar in ten minutes. He hoped it was going to be a quiet night. He could really use one, with everything going on with Velma. On the other hand, quiet nights never brought in much money.

He opened the cash register and made sure there were enough singles and five-dollar bills, as well as change, in the drawer. He then looked below the bar to make sure that everything was in place. There was enough liquor in the bottles. Suddenly, there was a knock at the door. *Already?* Don thought, looking at his watch. It was 5:25.

He walked over and unlocked the door. "Hello, Mr. Schein," he said to the older gentleman who ran the local pharmacy.

"Don, good to see you, young man," Mr. Schein said. "Where is mother?"

"Oh, she's not feeling well," said Don. "I'm tending bar for her tonight."

"Ach, what is wrong?" asked Mr. Schein. "I have my usual."

"I don't know," said Don, taking a Pabst Blue Ribbon out of the icebox, prying off the top on the bottle opener attached to the wall and pouring it into a glass. "She won't tell me. But she has a really nasty cough," he said, sliding the glass across the bar to Mr. Schein. "That's sixty-five cents, please."

"She should not be fooling around with that cough," said Mr. Schein, handing Don the change. "Not in this weather," he said, pointing to the window with his glass.

"Mr. Schein?" asked Don. "Do you think she should go to the doctor?"

"Yes, I do. With cough like that she should not let it go," said Mr. Schein.

"I think maybe she called the doctor but then never went to see him. The office called the bar and said Velma should call. But I don't think she ever did," said Don.

"Maybe she scared," Mr. Schein said. "Many people scared of doctors."

"Do you have anything at the store, sir, maybe that she could take for the cough?"

"Sure, I do! Sure. You come to store tomorrow, and I give to you," Mr. Schein said.

"Thank you, Mr. Schein. Thank you very much!" Don said, feeling better for having mentioned it.

"It's nothing," said Mr. Schein. "Tomorrow Saturday. You come by store tomorrow first thing."

"Yes, I will," said Don, looking at the door, which had just opened. Mrs. Olsen, wearing a blue overcoat and floral scarf tied at her chin, walked in carrying a shopping bag that she placed on the floor under the bar. She took her usual seat, the one closest to the window. "Don! Hello, boy. Where is mother?"

"Oh, she'll be back tomorrow," said Don. "She's not feeling well this evening."

"Not feeling well?" Mrs. Olsen asked. "I never see her not here! What is wrong?"

"Oh, she has a cold," said Don. "She's resting at home."

"I'll have a Rheingold, please. This cold," continued Mrs. Olsen, "everyone has it. You tell her she must drink lots of chicken soup and gargle with warm salt water every hour."

"Thank you, Mrs. Olsen," said Don. "I will tell her that. I'm sure she'll be very grateful."

"How are you, Mr. Schein?" asked Mrs. Olsen, turning to her right, where Mr. Schein was seated.

"God bless, everyone is well, thank you for asking," said Mr. Schein.

"And how are the children?" asked Mrs. Olsen, taking a sip from her glass of beer.

"Good, good!" Mr. Schein responded. "They work hard in school. I am very proud of them."

"How old are they now?" asked Mrs. Olsen, adjusting herself on her bar stool.

"William, he is eight and Frederick, he is ten years old," replied said Mr. Schein.

"Ah, those are good ages," said Mrs. Olsen, as she took another sip.

Don wiped down the bar with his rag and threw the bottles out in the trash. The door opened and Miriam walked in. She was the older daughter of the Friedkin family, and she was about Don's age, eighteen. She looked tired, with dark circles under her eyes, Don noticed.

"Hello, Miriam," said Don. "How are you doing?"

"Hello, Don. I'm okay. Is Velma here?" asked Miriam.

"No, she isn't here tonight. She's home sick in bed," said Don.

"Oh, I'm sorry to hear that. Don could I speak to you in private?" Miriam asked.

"Uh . . ." Don eyed the front door to see if more patrons were coming in. For the moment, the bar was quiet. "Sure. We can speak in the back room," Don said, coming out from behind the bar to meet Miriam.

When they got to Velma's office, Miriam said, "Don, my mother sent me because she needs a favor." Miriam looked down at the floor as she said this.

"What kind of favor?" asked Don, looking at her in the eye.

"Well, my father has disappeared again and my mother . . . well, she needs money for groceries. She was wondering if Velma could help her out with a few dollars," Miriam said.

"Oh," Don replied. He knew that Velma occasionally helped people out in the neighborhood when they couldn't pay their bills.

"Well, I could ask her, but I couldn't give you the money without her permission," said Don. "How much do you need?"

"She wanted me to ask for five dollars but, frankly, she'll take anything she can get."

"Well," Don said, reaching into his pocket, "I can lend your mother five dollars."

"You can?" asked Miriam.

"Yup, I have five dollars here," Don said, unrolling five single bills from a roll. "I made this running errands in the neighborhood this week. Take it."

"Oh, Don, thank you!" Miriam said, and put her hand on his shoulder. "I'll pay you back as soon as I can!"

"That's okay—don't worry about it. I know how it goes," said Don.

"Well, thanks again, Don. I won't forget it. And neither will my mother," said Miriam, and she walked down the length of the bar and out the door.

As Don looked after her it seemed she held her head higher than when she first walked into the bar.

CHAPTER EIGHTEEN

1956

Allison was leaning down, looking into the glass display of pastries at Glazer's Bake Shop. "I'll have an apple strudel, please," she said to the woman behind the counter, who was wearing a white apron and a hair net around her bun.

"One apple strudel it is. And for the young man?" the woman asked Don.

"Oh, let's see," said Don, surveying the choices, "could I please have a cheese Danish?" Turning to Allison, he said, "I can't believe you're leaving."

"I know," Allison said, looking at Don. "I can't believe I'm leaving either."

"Are you nervous?" asked Don, taking her hand.

"I am," Allison responded. "I've never lived away from home."

"Whose idea was it for you to go away to college?" asked Don.

"Well . . . my mother always wanted me to continue my studies. She didn't want me to just graduate from high school and get married. And she thought that St. Mary's College for Women would be the perfect place for me. I'm thinking about becoming a nurse."

"A nurse," Don repeated. "Wow, but Westchester County . . . geez, that seems really far away."

"Actually, it's not that far away at all," Allison said. "There's a bus and train that you can take and it's only about an hour. I can come home on weekends."

"I guess so," said Don, as he held the door open for her.

"Besides, it'll be good for me to get away," said Allison, as they turned the corner and walked down 86th Street toward the river.

"So, it wasn't only your mother's decision," said Don.

"Well, she was the one who originally brought it up," said Allison, "but the more I thought about it, the more I realized how much I'd like to try something new and have the opportunity to have adventures."

"Adventures," mused Don.

"Yes, adventures," continued Allison. "I love my family and I like our neighborhood, but I do the same things every day. Go to school, come home, do homework, help with chores, have dinner, go to sleep. Then, I get up in the morning and do it all over again. And on the weekends, I go to see my grandmother. I'd like to see *different* places, try something new," she said, as she brushed some strudel crumbs off her navy blue dress.

"Yeah, I guess I see your point," said Don, as he put the last bite of Danish into his mouth. "God knows I do the same thing day after day."

They had reached East End Avenue and 86th Street and were walking across the flagstones at the entrance to Carl Schurz Park. It was a warm spring day, and the sun was shining.

"Let's go sit by the water," Allison said.

"I'd like that," Don replied. They found a bench overlooking the East River and sat quietly for a few minutes.

"Don?" asked Allison, as she looked at a dark red tugboat making its way south along the water.

"Yeah?" Don responded.

"I don't want you to resent my leaving . . ." she said.

"No, no, I understand," Don said, looking at a building across the river in Queens.

"Do you?" Allison asked. "Do you, *really?*" The tugboat was almost out of her view.

"Sure, it's just . . ." he paused.

"Yes?" Allison asked.

"Well," Don began, "I'm really going to miss you," he said, turning towards her and kissing her on the mouth. Allison placed her hand on the back of his head as she kissed him back. "And I'm going to miss you, too. Come, let's walk," she said, as they got up and began walking along the esplanade.

"You realize I'm only going be an hour away," Allison continued, turning to Don as they walked. "I'll come home to visit. And you can visit me, too."

"Yeah, I guess so," said Don.

"Besides," she said, "you could use some excitement in your life, as well."

"Hmmm," Don mused, "excitement. I've never really thought about that."

"Well, think about it," said Allison. "How long have you been here?"

"My whole life," answered Don, as he looked at the island on the other side of the river with a building that looked like a hospital on it.

"Exactly my point," said Allison. "And where else have you been?"

"Not many places, really," said Don, slowly.

"That's what I'm talking about," said Allison. "Don't you want to see other places? What about travel? You could have your own adventures!"

"My own adventures . . ." Don repeated.

"Can I tell you something?" asked Allison, as they walked to the railing and leaned over to look at the water.

"Sure," said Don.

"I don't think you've ever had the time to think about your own needs," said Allison.

"Well, wait a minute," Don said as he faced Allison. "What do you mean?" he asked.

"I *mean*," continued Allison, "you go to school, then you help Velma at the bar, then you do your homework. I mean, haven't you ever wondered what you would do with a day off to yourself? When you could just do anything you pleased?

Haven't you ever wondered what that would feel like?"

"I guess I haven't really had the chance to," Don replied.

"Exactly!" proclaimed Allison. "That's what I'm saying. Wouldn't it be nice, for once, for you to have the chance to think about doing something for yourself? And I don't mean just a few hours off on Saturdays."

"Gee, I suppose so," said Don. "I've really never looked at it from that point of view."

"Well, I think it's about time that you start," said Allison. "What do you think? Look, it's a beautiful day and we're out here together. There's no one to bother us right now. Isn't this a great day to start having some dreams of your own?"

"Dreams," Don said.

"Yes, dreams," said Allison.

"Well," he continued, "I've always wondered what it would be like to live in the country."

"Okay," Allison responded. "That's a start."

"And I like small towns," Don continued. "Once, my uncle Sergei took us upstate—to the Catskills—to visit a friend of his, and he lived near a small town. I really liked that little town. I'd like to live in a town like that one day."

"Now you're talking," said Allison.

"And I really like the ocean," Don went on. "We went to Coney Island once. That was so much fun!"

"And . . ." continued Allison.

"And, what?" asked Don.

"And," Allison went on, "I noticed you didn't mention the one thing you love to do in your spare time."

"Oh," Don responded, "sketching!"

"Yes, dummy," Allison replied playfully, hitting him on the top of his head.

"Yeah, sketching," Don said. "I feel like I can't take it seriously, not as a job, at least."

"Why not?" Allison asked.

"Oh, you know, Velma and Sergei." Don replied. "They don't think art school is a realistic choice for me."

"Again, I ask," Allison challenged, "Why not?"

"Because they think I need to get a *real* job," Don stated.

"Well," Allison replied, "last time you mentioned Mr. Ballard, you said there were jobs as illustrators and cartoonists and draftspeople available."

"Yes, he did say that," Don said.

"Don," Allison demanded, "look at me."

Don turned and looked in Allison's eyes.

"It's your life," she continued, "not theirs. If there are jobs available and you can train for them it's your job to figure out how to do that. You'll never be happy taking some job just because it's practical. I know you want more than that for yourself."

"Yes, I suppose you're right," Don said, leaning over and kissing Allison on the mouth.

"See?" asked Allison, when they stopped. "You *do* have dreams," she said as they leaned back and watched a large red barge slowly float down the river.

CHAPTER NINETEEN

1956

About a month later, Don locked the door to the bar and walked over to the Ideal Restaurant for dinner. He had taken to treating himself to a meal out on the nights he had to work the bar. This got him out of the habit of just eating a sandwich brought from home while he worked.

It was beginning to get chilly for early October and Don realized he had worn the wrong jacket. He pulled the zipper up closer to the top of his collar and hunched his shoulders a bit as he turned the corner and walked into the brisk Second Avenue wind.

At 86th Street, he turned left and stopped in Elk Candy to pick up some marzipan fruit for dessert. In the Ideal, he took a seat at the counter towards the back, right before the stairs that led to the table seating area.

"Hello, Don!" said an older blond woman behind the counter. "How good to see you! How is mother? You have your 'usual?'"

"Oh, hello Mrs. Becker. Thanks. Yes, she's

fine," said Don. "Doing much better after she got over pneumonia."

"Ach, we were all so worried about her last winter. This is nothing to fool around with, this pneumonia," Mrs. Becker said.

"No, it sure isn't," said Don. "She had me really worried."

"Oh, yes, I can only imagine," said Mrs. Becker. "And it is only you and she. That must be frightening for a young man."

"Yes, it was," said Don, who was about to take off his jacket, then thought better of it, as he felt a draft coming from the front door.

"Here it is," Mrs. Becker said, sliding Don's usual, a roast beef on rye with onion and mustard, over the counter to him. "What to drink, Don?"

"Oh, I'll have some black coffee, please," he said.

Don pulled out a folded copy of *The Daily News* from his back pocket and began to read the sports pages. There were some people sitting a few stools over from Don, a man and a woman, talking in low voices. As Don sipped the coffee Mrs. Becker had put down on the counter, he continued to read the paper. Then he looked up. He thought he heard the name "Velma" mentioned. Don put down the paper and started eating his sandwich, trying to turn his head slightly so that he could hear the couple's conversation better. Looking up, he realized he could see their reflection in the mirror behind the back counter. The man looked like he was in his early thirties, and the woman, who was younger, was probably in her mid twenties. He had dark hair, combed back, and was wearing a brown suit and maroon tie. She had auburn hair that fell below her shoulders and had on red lipstick and a wine-colored dress.

Finishing up his sandwich, Don asked for his check and decided to use the bathroom at the back of the restaurant. When he returned, he walked past the couple and noticed that they bowed their heads to drink their coffee as he walked by.

"Goodbye, Mrs. Becker," said Don, as he paid his bill, and made his way to the front door.

"You send my best to mother," said Mrs. Becker. "Bye-bye!"

As Don closed the door behind him, he held his package of marzipan and felt his chest tightening. Walking back along 86th Street to Second Avenue he thought about the couple. He could have sworn he heard them say the name "Velma".

Instead of turning right on Second Avenue, Don decided to duck into the vestibule of the apartment building on the corner. He pulled out his newspaper, unfolding it so his face was hidden while he read. After a few minutes he lowered the paper just an inch and saw the couple walk by towards Second Avenue. Don folded the paper, put it in his back pocket, and followed the couple as they turned right onto Second Avenue.

They crossed 85th Street, then continued to the corner of 84th where they stopped and looked around. They stood there talking for a few minutes, then crossed 84th Street and continued down Second Avenue. Don watched them until they were far down the avenue, then he crossed the street and headed to the bar.

When he got there, he let himself in and locked the door behind him, placing the marzipan on the bar.

He looked at the clock: 5:00 p.m. He had plenty of time to set up. Walking to the back room, he pulled out a pack of Lucky Strikes—a recent habit—from his pocket and struck a match against the table to light his cigarette. Sitting down at the desk, he opened the window and stared at the tall weeds in the yard that faced Velma's. He pulled the chair over from the desk and sat down to smoke as he stared out at the world beyond the back window.

A child was crying, the couple upstairs was fighting, as usual. Somewhere, someone was cooking beef. Sounds. Don heard so many different sounds in the city. He seemed to hear less these days. He felt like he heard more of them when he was little. Were there more sounds or was he listening less?

The sounds of the city made their own kind of music. There were the sounds of newspapers, piles of them tied up with string and dropped on the ground when the neighborhood kids gathered them for scrap drives during the war. There were the sounds of metal garbage cans being hauled across the sidewalk for trash pickup day.

And there were the sounds of a summer day when Don was around six years old, and Velma let him play in the fire hydrant with the other kids on 82nd Street. It was hot, hovering somewhere around ninety degrees, and the corner apartment which faced south and west, was unbearable. It was a Sunday, and the bar was closed. There was nothing to do but sit outside and wait for the heat to pass. Velma brought a cushion down and sat on the stoop, talking to her neighbor, Mrs. Oblensky, while Don and the other kids from the block ran in and out of the fire hydrant, screaming with joy. He didn't remember another time that he had so much fun. The water was bracingly cold and so refreshing, after the heat of the sun. Most of the boys were in their underwear and the girls were in their dresses.

Afterwards, the boys played stickball, using the manhole covers in the street as bases. The girls got their jump ropes out and started a game of Double Dutch. Later all the parents gave their children money so they could have ice cream from the Good Humor truck. As the sun set, around 9:00 p.m., Don came home, hot, sticky and exhausted. Velma made him rinse off in the tub, then he collapsed into his bed, passing out immediately.

And there were the sounds that were less like music and more like minor explosions that erupted out of nowhere on May 8th, 1945. Don was pulling down the chairs at the bar, when he heard a massive rumbling of voices, screams, and what sounded like spoons against metal pots.

"What is this?" Velma asked, wiping her hands on her dress and going to the front door. When she stepped out into the sunshine, there were people everywhere, cheering and chanting, blowing horns and banging on cans.

"It's over! The war is over!" folks were screaming. Children were jumping in the air.

"Ach, bojemoy, could this be true?" Velma asked, taking it all in.

"It's true!" Mr. Smolnecki honked from his Checker cab, as he parked in front of the bar. "It was just announced on the radio!"

Velma looked at the sky and started to cry.

"Ma, are you okay?" Don asked, concerned.

"My Dontchik," Velma said, pulling him close. "I weep tears of joy."

Don took his last drag and stubbed out his cigarette on the outside of the window sill. He looked at the clock on the wall: it was 5:15. He'd better get started. Velma would join him at 5:30. She had taken to coming in when the bar opened, asking Don to set up for her when she was still sick. It had taken her several months to get back to full health again and Don would get the bar ready for her, then he would help her serve as soon as she arrived.

As he counted the bills in the register, he wondered about that childhood summer and the feeling of running around the hydrant with his friends. *Whatever happened to those days?* Don wondered, placing the last single under the clip that held the bills in place.

There was the familiar knock on the door and Don went around the bar to open it and let Velma in.

"Dontchik, you count money?" she asked, as she stepped in, closing and locking the door behind her.

"Yes, Ma," he replied, going back behind the bar, to make sure there was enough change in the register.

"You polish glasses?" Velma asked, removing her light wool coat, and hanging it on the hook in the back room.

"Yes, Ma," Don said, placing a clean rag in his back pocket for wiping down the bar throughout the night.

"You count beer?"

"Yes, Ma," Don rolled his eyes, out of Velma's sight.

"Okay, you good boy," she said, ruffling his hair.

"Ma!" he exclaimed, trying to escape her grasp.

"Ach, Dontchik, you so big," she said. "I no recognize you!"

It was 5:30. Velma walked over to the front door and unlocked it. As the patrons started coming and the bell on the door kept ringing Don quickly forgot about summer fire hydrants as he got to work serving the locals. Around 6:00 p.m., when the smoke was thick and the conversation lively, the door opened, and a couple walked in. Don looked up from the beer he was pouring and immediately recognized the man and woman from the Ideal Restaurant. He tried to stay focused on keeping the Schlitz he was pouring from spilling, but he could not get the image of this couple uttering Velma's name out of his head. Don stayed at the back of the bar, having Velma work the front, as much as he could. The couple walked to the back and the woman leaned over the bar.

"Why, hello there," she said, smiling at Don.

"Hello," he said, reluctantly.

"Haven't I seen you somewhere?" she asked.

"Nope, don't think so," Don lied. "Here ya go," he said, as he slid a Pabst Blue Ribbon across the counter to a patron.

"No?" she asked. "I thought maybe I just saw you having a sandwich at the Ideal, on 86th Street," she said. "You looked a little lonely."

Don looked at her. "What can I get you?" he asked.

"Oh, well, I'd love a beer," the woman responded.

"Schlitz or Pabst Blue Ribbon?" Don asked.

"Schlitz, please," she said. "Oh, and another one for my friend, too."

"Right," said Don, retrieving the bottles and opening them on the wall.

"Here's a dollar," the woman said, as she placed the bill on the bar and looked into Don's eyes. "Keep the change."

"Thanks," Don replied, trying not to get excited. Getting a tip this large was rare at Velma's.

Luckily, the bar was busy that evening and Don had to serve lots of customers, not just this couple.

"Say," the woman said a little later, "how's about you and me have a little drink together later? I'd like to get to know you a little," she said, putting her hand on Don's, as he wiped spilled beer off the bar.

"Dontchik!" Velma called, from the front end of the bar.

"Excuse me," Don said to the young woman and walked down the back of the bar to Velma.

"Dontchik," Velma said in his hear, "who is this girl? What she want with you?"

"I don't know, Ma. They were in the Ideal, when I was having dinner before," Don decided against telling Velma he thought he heard them mention her name.

"I don't like this," said Velma. "This no good."

"It's okay, Ma, I can handle her," Don said.

"Dontchik, you give me signal, if you need my help," Velma said.

"Sure, ma. Thanks," he said, and went back to serving the customers.

By now, the couple had taken two seats that had been previously occupied at the end of the bar and the girl kept her eyes on Don, as she drank her beer and spoke to her companion.

"Don," she asked, "could I have another Schlitz, please?" looking deeply into his eyes.

"Yup," said Don, irritated that she called him by name. He opened the icebox and pulled out another bottle of Schlitz.

"Dontchik," said Velma, as she approached from the other end of the bar, "you work front."

"Sure, Ma," said Don, relieved to get away from the young woman and her stare.

"Everything good?" Velma asked the couple.

"Sure, fine," the man responded.

"I no see you here before," said Velma. "You new in neighborhood?"

"Oh, we're just passing by," the man said.

"'Passing by?' From where?" asked Velma, as she handed one of the regulars a bottle of Pabst Blue Ribbon.

"Oh, uh, we're from Long Island, here to have some dinner and take in a show," the man responded.

"Good, I tell you where to go," said Velma and, as Don watched, launched into a directive about all the right places to eat and be entertained on 86th Street. For the next half hour, Velma guarded her turf at the back, while the couple finished their beers and eventually got up to leave.

"Bye, Don," the woman called, as they walked to the front of the bar. "See ya around sometime," she said as she gave him a wink before they opened the door and walked out.

CHAPTER TWENTY

1956

Don lay on the living room couch in his pajamas, listening to the pelting rain against the window.

In his hand he held a letter from Allison. *"Dear Don,"* it began, *"I have some really bad news . . ."* She went on to say that she was moving, suddenly, back to Ireland. She did not think this would be a permanent move, but she wasn't sure when she would be back. Her father's sister had suddenly taken ill, and she had a new baby. The family had written, asking if Allison's mother could come and help, for a period of time. Allison saw no reason why she could not stay at St. Mary's and finish out her studies, but her mother had categorically refused. "So, for the foreseeable future," Allison had written "I'll be writing to you from County Clare, rather than County Westchester."

Don appreciated that Allison was trying to make light of the situation, but he was not amused. He felt heavy and confused. Allison had come to mean so much to him and he felt calm when he was with her.

There was no one that he knew that he could talk to the way he could talk to Allison.

Don worried about what Allison was going to do in Ireland, helping out her family as a housekeeper and nursemaid, when she was used to being an independent young woman at an American college.

He sat up and looked out the window again. It was still raining. Everything was so strange. So much was happening all at the same time. Allison's news. Then there was the business with Velma and Sergei, who were disturbed after the time the man followed Don to the bar. Suddenly, there were hushed conversations, in which Don heard words like *leave town*, and *escape*.

He got up, dressed, found his jacket and an umbrella, and left the house, lighting a cigarette in the vestibule of the building. As Don walked out and turned south on Third Avenue, he opened his umbrella and listened to the rain against it. He had no particular destination in mind. He just needed to walk.

At 79th Street, Don passed by Rappaport Toy Shop and stopped in front of the window to look at the train display. He'd always wanted a set like the one in the window when he was little and once, for Christmas, Sergei had given him a small one with several feet of circular track and three small cars— an engine, one for passengers, and a caboose. Don treasured this set and played with it for years. He still had it in his closet in its original box. He stared at the trains, while smoking his cigarette and wondered about the places that trains could take you to—mountains, oceans, prairies.

Don could count on one hand the number of trips he had taken in his life. As a small boy, around age four, he had gone upstate with Velma and Sergei to Hudson, to visit some friends from the bar. They had insisted that everyone come to visit their "dacha" in the country. Finally, Sergei convinced Velma that the fresh air would do everyone some good and Velma had relented, leaving an associate of Sergei's in charge of the bar for that Friday and Saturday. In Grand Central, Don walked through the small hallway into the massive main hall. He could not stop staring at the cavernous ceiling, walking with his hand in Velma's and his head up, almost bumping into someone in the process. "Dontchik! Look where you going!" she scolded him.

On the train, he stared out the window for the whole ride at the majestic Hudson River and the Palisades on the other side. At Georgi and Caterina's cottage, Don ran around in the grass, tossing stones in the stream and gathering wood for the fire at night.

The only other trip was when Don was nine. Sergei borrowed a car from his friend, Sasha, and drove Velma and Don to the beach. The wind blew in Don's hair as he stuck his head out the window while Sergei sailed down Flatbush Avenue, past Ebbet's Field, in Brooklyn. In the Rockaways, Don ate popcorn and Sergei rented bicycles on the boardwalk, showing Don how to ride. When he put his feet into the water, Don felt like a new person. Sergei held his hand while Velma nervously watched him from the shore.

"The boy must learn to swim," Sergei later told Velma. "It is not a choice," he warned her. "I will take care of this," and arranged for Don to take swimming lessons that summer at the public pool in Yorkville. Now, Don was grateful. He knew so many kids who couldn't swim. It would be awful to be at the beach and have to sit out of the water.

Don wondered why he and Allison had never gone to the beach together. They could have taken the train to Coney Island. Don pictured the perfect summer day, eating hot dogs on the boardwalk, swimming in cool water, and watching Allison's dark hair blowing in the wind. Later they would lie in the sand, looking up and seeing nothing but sky overhead.

The rain had stopped, and the sun shone against the wet pavement. Don closed his umbrella and looked up. He couldn't believe how bright it was. Now that there was no more elevated subway, Third Avenue was positively lit up when the sun was out.

CHAPTER TWENTY-ONE

1957

Last Call: Free Beer!

The sign was posted on the window of the bar and several of the regulars were staring at it in disbelief. "I cannot believe she is closing," Mr. Schein was saying. "This was, how they say, my home away from home."

Mrs. Olsen said, "Every day at 5:30, I came here on the way home. I knew everyone here. If I go somewhere else, I won't see all the familiar faces."

"Why is she closing?" Mr. Schein was asking. "I don't understand why she is closing."

"I heard it's for her health," said Mrs. Olsen. "The doctor told her she has to go out West where there is clean air for her lungs. Which is nonsense. Everyone knows she never went to see doctors. She didn't believe in them!"

Don unlocked the door and Mr. Schein and Mrs. Olsen started walking in. "Don, this is such sad day," said Mr. Schein. "I will really miss you and Velma."

"I know, I'll miss you, too," said Don, looking away from Mr. Schein.

"Hello, Mrs. Olsen," said Don, as he closed the door behind her.

"Don, I can't believe it," said Mrs. Olsen, as she walked over to the bar to take her regular seat. "Is today really the last day?"

"I'm afraid it is," Don answered. He slid open the cooler door to get out beer bottles, a Pabst Blue Ribbon for Mr. Schein and a Rheingold for Mrs. Olsen.

"Are Velma and Sergei really moving out West?" asked Mrs. Olsen.

"Yes, the doctor says Velma needs a different climate," said Don.

"Really?" asked Mrs. Olsen. "Don, is this the real story?"

"Yes, Mrs. Olsen, that's the real story," said Don. Another patron walked in. "Oh, hello, Mr. Smolnecki, thanks for coming by."

"Don, you still need me to fix the broken latch in the bathroom?" he asked.

"Yes, the door doesn't lock right now," said Don.

"Okay, I go fix it now," said Mr. Smolnecki, as he walked to the back of the bar.

"Thank you, Mr. Smolnecki. Then you can have your beer!" Don winked at him.

"Yes, my reward. Free beer!" Mr. Smolnecki responded, smiling as he walked to the small bathroom located right before the back room.

Velma came out from her office, just as Mr. Smolnecki was opening the door to the bathroom. "Thank you for fix this, Mr. Smolnecki," Velma said, and went behind the bar.

"Velma! This is a sad day," called Mrs. Olsen from the front of the bar. "The neighborhood will not be the same without you."

"Yes, I am sad, too," said Velma, "but it is for my health." She looked away, as she picked up a clean rag to wipe down the bar.

"And why so far away?" asked Mrs. Olsen, as she lit a cigarette and sipped her Rheingold.

"The doctor says I need better climate," said Velma. "The air in New York no good for me."

"Ah, clean air," Mrs. Olsen repeated. "This sounds nice. Maybe, one day, I'll have clean air, too."

"I heard they had to leave town," Mr. Schein said under his breath to Mrs. Olsen.

"Yes, I heard something like this, too," Mrs. Olsen responded.

"They couldn't make it work here anymore," Mr. Schein continued. "Too many pressures from the outside."

"The neighborhood is changing," said Mrs. Olsen, as she took a drag on her cigarette and stared out the window.

"Yes, it is," Mr. Schein responded.

"Dontchik, we need more beer!" Velma called out.

"Sure, Ma!" Don responded. "Mr. Smolnecki,"

Don yelled, as he walked to the back. "Can you help me out?"

"Yes, of course," Mr. Smolnecki said, putting down his tools in the back room, as he and Don headed out to the street to open the cellar doors.

As they hauled the beer back up the stairs, Don saw a group of musicians, the Triple Trio—Helga, Martin and Joseph—coming through the door, with their instruments in their hands.

"Velma!" Helga called, as she burst in the door.

"Helga!" Velma responded, putting down her rag and coming out from behind the bar to hug Helga.

"You cannot be really closing this bar!" Helga said.

"Yes, my dear, I am sorry. Tonight is last night," Velma said, handing a Rheingold to a gentleman in overalls and a Fedora.

"No!" exclaimed Helga, "I refuse to believe it!"

"Here," Velma said, handing Helga, Martin and Joseph their beers. "To your health!"

"No!" yelled Helga. "To yours!" and the trio raised their glasses to Velma.

"Everyone! Listen!" Helga called out and the voices in the bar started to quiet down. "Tonight is a sad night for the neighborhood. Velma's—this is an institution!" Everyone raised their beer bottles and cheered.

"Once there was a tavern 'round the corner . . ." Helga started singing. Martin joined in on the violin, and Joseph began beating his tambourine.

Before long, all the patrons in the bar were singing with the trio. In the back, Mr. Smolnecki was finished and putting his tools away while a young couple had started dancing, somehow spinning each other in the small space between the bar and the door to the back room.

The smoke was rising and so were the patrons' spirits. Before long, a couple of burly New York City police officers walked in and, after getting their Rheingolds, raised them in the air. "Ah, Velma, we're sure going to miss you!" they shouted. Don took a moment to stop and look around. In his memory, there had never been a night like this.

As the evening wore on, more and more patrons kept pouring into the bar until the beer ran out. "Friends, we've run out of beer," Don announced. "We'll be serving the hard stuff until we're done." A cheer went up from the crowd.

Around 9:30, Sergei walked in, dressed in a dark blue suit and grey felt hat. "It looks like a very lively crowd," he loudly commented to Don.

"Yes," Don answered. "And we've run out of beer."

"Ah, yes. You are serving the liquor now, I presume?" Sergei asked.

"Yes, we're almost done with that, too."

"Good," Sergei said, "what you do now is you make an announcement that the liquor is almost gone and that the bar will close at 10:00."

"But everyone is having such a good time," Don protested.

"They won't be having such a 'good time' when the liquor runs out, Don," Sergei stated.

"Okay," said Don, as he made his way behind the bar to take out the last bottle of vodka.

Later, after the last patron had left and Sergei had taken Velma home, Don wiped down the bar and put up the chairs, leaving one out for himself. He then lit a cigarette and sat down at the bar. As he smoked, he looked around. With it empty, the silence was overwhelming.

Finally, Don got up, replaced the stool, and unlocked the door to let himself out, glancing around one last time. It occurred to him that he would never do this again. He would never open or close this door or the one to the cellar. This would be the last time he walked home from the bar on 84th Street.

CHAPTER TWENTY-TWO

1957

Stepping out under the night sky, Don stared at the massive trail of stars overhead.

Striking his match against the doorframe he sat down in the rocker on the small front porch. He didn't remember seeing as much light in his whole life as he had on this trip out west. He looked at the stars and couldn't believe how bright the Big Dipper was. Had he ever seen a sky like this? He did remember Georgi and Sergei pointing out various stars to him when they went to the Catskills together but that was the only time. Don never saw the stars in the city.

The bus ride to Whitefish had been short and bearable. Don had arrived feeling somewhat rested, after his stopover in Missoula, as well as anxious about seeing Velma and Sergei.

"Dontchik, it is beautiful, no?" Velma asked, coming out to join him. She sat down in the rocker opposite him.

"It sure is," Don said. They sat in silence for a

period of time, looking at the snow-capped mountains in the distance.

"Dontchik," Velma finally said. "You must be so tired. Come, I show you your room," and they got up to go inside.

Don looked around at the log cabin that Sergei had rented. It had wood paneling and rustic furniture and there was a fire burning in the living room. "This way," said Velma, leading Don up the small staircase to the left.

At the top of the stairs, there was a narrow hallway with entrances to two bedrooms. The room at the back faced the mountains and it was filled with sunlight. "What you think?" Velma asked excitedly.

"Wow," Don stood looking around at the room that was furnished with a wooden bed, dresser and small armchair. "Ma, it's something else. I don't know what to say . . ."

"Never did we see so much sun in New York, yes?" Velma asked. "Dontchik, you have something to eat, then you can lie down."

There was the sound of footsteps coming up the stairs. "Well, Don," Sergei came in, wearing a dark blue flannel shirt and khaki pants. He gave Don a big hug. "You made it. I hope the trip was uneventful. It's good to see you."

"Yes, well, I am starting to feel really tired suddenly. I do think I'll lie down for a bit," he said, looking longingly at the bed.

"You no want to eat now, Dontchik?" Velma asked.

"No, Ma, I can wait," Don replied.

"Okay, we go," said Velma. "Come Sergei," she said, as they walked out of the room, closing the door behind them.

Don sat down on the side of the bed, took his shoes off, then lay down on his back. The mattress was the most delightful one he had ever come in contact with. It was soft and firm, all at the same time, and for the moment, Don pictured never leaving it. Perhaps he could stay in bed for three days, just emerging for meals, then go back to sleep. He lay back and looked at the pitched ceiling. How different it was from the flat, cracked one in Yorkville. Don closed his eyes and saw himself floating on a cloud, drifting through a massive sky, directionless, just letting the cloud take him on its path.

When he woke up at 6:00 p.m. he wasn't sure where he was. The October light had changed, and the room was filled with the rays of the low setting sun. Don looked outside. The sky had turned a warm orange. He opened the window and smelled the cool mountain air.

"Dontchik, come set table for dinner," Velma called.

Don sat up, stretched his arms, and swung his legs over the bed to put his shoes back on.

"You want cup of tea, Dontchik?" Velma asked, as Don came into the kitchen and sat down at the small table in the corner.

"Yes, thank you, that would be great," said Don, stretching his arms once more to wake up.

Dinner was simple—chicken cutlets and potatoes, with green beans on the side. "And for dessert," Velma said, "I make your favorite apple turnover."

"What?" Don was incredulous, "Ma, you haven't made this for ages!"

"Yes, I know," Velma responded. "Now, I have time!"

As they were finishing their dessert Sergei drank his tea and took a deep breath. "Don," he began, "we are very happy you have made it here safely. We are hoping that you can see a life for yourself out here, the way your mother and I are planning."

Don looked at Sergei. "You know, I was followed in Minneapolis."

"What?!" Velma said.

"Don, you should have told me," said Sergei.

"Short guy. Unpleasant eyes," Don said.

"I must look into this," Sergei said.

"Yeah, well, I shook him," said Don. "It may have been a coincidence." Then he paused. "So, this is it? You're staying here? For good?"

"Well, Don, this is not just 'it', as you say," said Sergei. "This was a massive undertaking, closing down the bar and the operation and moving out here."

"Yes, I can appreciate that, but what are you going to do out here? Start all over?" Don asked.

"In a matter of speaking, yes, we are thinking of starting all over," said Sergei. "The operation could very well work out here. There is a community of working people, to say nothing of tourists, and everyone likes a good bar."

"Okay," Don said.

"You see, Don, we had to move our business out of town. We were being muscled in on by forces that would have made our lives, especially your mother's, very difficult," said Sergei. "The police, the Health Department, they were easy. After all, everyone likes a drink."

"Uh huh," Don replied.

"It was the other element—the local mob, the syndicate, whatever you want to call it—that was the difficult part. I couldn't have you or your mother threatened while you were working. You can understand that, can't you?"

"Yes, I can," Don responded.

"I am glad to hear that, Don. I am hoping that means that you will join us here and help us start our new life in this beautiful place. After all, I think all you have to do is look around to see how good things could be here."

Don paused to think about what Sergei was saying. "For the moment, I think I need a cigarette under the stars," he said, and got up to leave the table, clearing his dessert dishes on the way.

"Yes, of course," said Sergei, getting up to help Velma with the dishes.

Outside, Don sat down on the porch and pulled a package of Lucky Strikes from his shirt pocket. He lit one up and smoked while staring up at the velvety sky.

Sergei's proposal was not what Don had expected. He thought he was going to meet Velma and Sergei to deliver the money, they would spend some time out West—which was what they had told him—and that they would return to another part of the city, perhaps downtown, in the Village where Sergei had his place. The trip was never proposed to him as a final destination. Perhaps they were scared Don would share the information with someone and the word would get out?

Don finished his cigarette and took another look up at the sky. The vastness of it overwhelmed him and he suddenly felt a bit dizzy, as if even sitting down by the cabin he couldn't get his bearings. He got up and went back inside, thinking he was ready to turn in.

"I'm going to head up to bed, now," Don said. "Thanks for the delicious meal, Ma."

"Good night, my boy," said Velma, kissing Don on his forehead.

"Good night, Don," Sergei said, "I hope you sleep well in your new bed."

"Good night," Don said as he made his way up the small staircase to the top floor.

As he undressed and crawled into the bed, pulling the fluffy duvet across him, Don wondered whether he could make a life for himself here. Could he live in the country, having grown up in the city where he could walk anywhere he wanted or hop on the subway? He didn't know how to drive, and in order to live in a place like this he would have to get his driver's license and buy a car.

And what about Allison? He didn't know if he would see her anytime soon, but he couldn't imagine that he would never see her again. He knew that they would have some kind of future together—he just didn't know where or when.

Don looked out the window at the star-filled sky. It certainly was beautiful here. He wondered about the next phase of his life. Where would it take place?

CHAPTER TWENTY-THREE

1957

Don stared out the train window and wondered what to do next.

The Empire Builder was making its way across eastern Montana, where the landscape had changed from the mountains and lakes of Whitefish to the open prairie. It was serene, with grasses and wind dancing in their own time across a slate-blue sky where enormous clouds simply sat.

Don could read his book, or he could take a nap. He couldn't remember the last time he had so much freedom on his hands. And space. There was so much of it in Montana that Don did not quite know what to make of it, coming from a neighborhood where there was rarely enough of it. At first, he loved spending time outdoors, breathing in the clean mountain air and just taking it all in—the breathtaking views, the gentle colors, the open sky. Sergei had taken Don around the area to show him the sights—they had rented bikes, gone hiking on Big Mountain and inquired about ski lessons for

Don. Sergei skied but had little time in New York to do so. Now, he was taking advantage of the opportunity to ski again in the coming months and introduce Don to the sport, as well.

As the weeks went by, though, Don, started to feel a little disoriented. When he went out, he found himself overwhelmed by what seemed like a constant wind and the amount of space around him. He liked walking in town but when they drove on the open roads outside of Whitefish, he felt almost dizzy, as if he didn't know where he was or what would ground him.

In these moments, he found himself thinking about New York, where there had been so little space. The bar was closed, and it wouldn't be his center anymore. For his whole life, Don had walked the streets of Yorkville, from the apartment to school, to the bar, and all the other locations he had frequented, with never a thought that one day it would all come to an end. He even wondered about the patrons, and how they were doing right now. Where was Miriam's mother going to get the money to buy her groceries while waiting for her husband to come home? And what about Mr. Smolnecki, who was saving up to take a trip upstate, but didn't want to drink away his savings? Mrs. Olsen would need the money for her niece's dance lessons, wouldn't she?

Don reflected on the service Velma and Sergei had provided the community for all those years. He remembered how, as a boy, he never understood the phrase "for the house" until the operation was uncovered by others. When he was older, and the shifty characters in the neighborhood started to become a threat, Sergei had called Don downtown to his apartment for a talk.

"Have a seat," Sergei said, motioning to the couch, as Don came into the living room. "Can I make you some tea?" Sergei asked.

"Yes, please," Don responded, as Sergei went into the kitchen.

"Here you are," Sergei said as he returned with a small tray, two cups and saucers, a creamer and sugar bowl. Sergei poured Don a cup of tea and joined him on the couch. "I brought you down here because I wanted to talk to you about some changes that are happening for all of us. I am thinking that we need to move away from New York City," he said, as he watched Don's face to see how he would respond. Don, stunned, put his teacup down on its saucer.

"What we have been doing all these years in New York is not working anymore and that's why it is coming to an end, Don," he began. "People in our communities, as you know, have often had trouble getting money from banks, so your mother and I have made it possible for them to have cash available for burying their dead, for a burial society that would allow them to pay for a funeral without being charged rates that they could not afford.

"Come—I want to show you something," said

Sergei, leading Don to the desk, as they put their teacups down on the coffee table. "These are the books, Don," he said, as he pulled a ledger from his desk drawer, "and you can see that the records have been meticulously maintained by Velma. She kept track of every penny that came in over the price of a beer or drink and wrote down every loan and deposit on a receipt. We had a good thing going for a long time, Don."

"My friend, Sasha, you know him from the bar—he sold me this building when we came to New York—and he has family and some land out in Montana. It's near a town called Whitefish, which is by Glacier National Park. He thinks it would be a perfect place for us to start over and for Velma to be in a better climate for her health."

"Don," Sergei said, "I want you to have something. I've been meaning to give this to you," and he handed Don a small, long box wrapped in brown paper. Don unwrapped it, opened the box and found a brown fountain pen inside.

"Oh, gee," Don said, examining the pen in his hand.

"I know you've always admired mine," Sergei said, "so I wanted you to have one of your own."

"Thank you, Sergei," Don said. "This is wonderful."

At first, Don didn't know what to make of Sergei's news. One part of him was elated—he would get to go out West and see the part of the country he had dreamt of and only seen on film. The other part was unsure—this wasn't turning into a visit. Sergei was talking about something much bigger.

The "good thing" Sergei had talked about . . . Don didn't know if it was good or not. It was just his life. He knew of no other. Now that it might be coming to an end, he wasn't sure how to feel. Whether it was good or not, he couldn't imagine doing anything else because he had never had the opportunity. Now that he did, he wasn't sure what to make of it. Sure, he had dreamed of traveling to different places, but now that he might actually be doing it, he felt strange, as if he was in an alien land.

Sergei proposed that he and Velma would travel together, and Don would come alone, several weeks later. Sergei felt that the bar had been watched for a long time, and that they might not be safe traveling together. He suggested that Don travel alone with the cash they would have left over after they repaid the bar patrons the money they had put into *the house*. At first Don wasn't sure about this—it seemed risky, and he didn't want to take on the responsibility for all that money. After mulling it over some more, though, the adventure of Sergei's proposal began to appeal to him. It made him feel important and he decided to go along with it.

Don was grateful for the train ride—Sergei had suggested it, after all the time he had spent on the bus—and the money Sergei had given him to take his trip to Ireland. "I hope you can see your way to coming back," he had said, as he handed him an envelope full of cash.

"Dontchik, I know you make right decision," Velma said, as she hugged Don, then turned away, dabbing at her eyes with her white handkerchief, at the train station.

Don had no idea what the right decision was. He only knew he needed some time to think things through.

CHAPTER TWENTY-FOUR

1957

As the Empire Builder continued towards Chicago, Don looked out the window at the nightime sky and thought about fireworks.

One Fourth of July, when Don was around twelve, Velma and Sergei were driving home from the West Side.

Sergei had taken the family to Riverside Park to watch the fireworks. It was still hot, and everyone was tired, but Don noticed something outside the car and craned his head out the open window.

"What's that?" Don asked, pointing at the top of a tenement on East 79th Street.

"What is it, Dontchik?" Velma asked, looking out the passenger side window to try and see where Don was pointing.

"Look, more fireworks!" Don exclaimed. "Up there!"

Velma looked out the window and saw what Don was looking at: fireworks shooting up into the sky from the roof of a tenement.

"Well, I see they have their own fireworks show up there," Sergei said.

"That's so neat!" Don cried, craning to look some more.

"Yes, it is neat," Sergei replied.

The following June, on the last Friday before the school year ended, Don overheard a conversation at school.

"Didja get it?" Fred asked, leaning over during math class.

"Yeah, I got it," Tomek answered.

"Gentleman, please stop talking," Mr. Stephens said sternly.

"I'll tell ya on the school yard. Hey Don, you want in?" Tomek asked.

"In what?" Don asked, looking up from his mathematics notebook.

"Gentleman!" Mr. Stephens raised his voice.

The boys all got back to work.

In the school yard, Tomek, Fred, and Joseph gathered together in a huddle.

"Okay," Tomek said. "I got the stuff from Mr. Giovanni's store. I got the fireworks and the sparklers."

Don was walking by.

"Hey, Don," Tomek said, "we got fireworks for the Fourth of July. You wanna set 'em off with us on the roof?"

Don was amazed. "Gee, that sounds . . ." He paused. "Lemme think about it. I don't know if my mom and uncle have something planned. I'll let you know."

"Okay, you let us know," Tomek said. "We do it every year. It's crazy!"

"Sure thing," Don said, wondering how on earth the boys got away with setting off fireworks on a roof. He started walking away, and then it hit him. Last summer, in the car, with Velma and Sergei. Fireworks on the roof.

That night, he lay in bed staring at the ceiling. He tried to go to sleep, but he kept thinking about the boys setting off fireworks on a roof. *Were Tomek, Fred, and Joseph the boys from the roof?* He thought some more. *Nah, they didn't live on 79th Street. So, there were other boys setting off fireworks?*

Was he in or out? Part of him thought this was a terrible idea—it probably wasn't safe, someone could get hurt, what if the cops found out? And another part of him was intrigued. How did they do it? Where did they get them? Did any parents know about this?

Certainly watching his friends set off fireworks would be more fun than going to Riverside Park with Velma, Sergei, and the locals from the neighborhood. He made a decision: tomorrow he would approach the boys and tell them he was going to join them. Yet even as he resolved to do this, he felt unsure. He couldn't possibly tell Velma or Sergei he was planning to set off some fireworks on the roof of a local building. At the same time, it sounded co-vert, like he would have to sneak around, something he never got a chance to do. He went back and forth for a minute then decided: he was in.

The next day, Don found Tomek, Fred, and Joseph on the school yard.

"Hey," Don asked, "you still planning on setting off fireworks on the Fourth?"

"Yeah," Tomek responded, "sure are. What about it? You in?"

"Yes!" Don said. "What time should I show up. And where?"

"Okay!" Tomek said. "Say you come by my house 'round about 6:00 p.m. 513 East 84th. Top floor. 5R."

"Deal!" Don proclaimed.

That afternoon, Don planned his speech to Velma. *Ma, I want to go to Tomek's house for the Fourth of July.* He pictured her response.

What, Dontchik? No, we go to park with Sergei.

I know, but this year I want to be with my friends.

But we always do this together.

But my friends, they asked me to go to their house and I want to go.

This would be harder than Don had planned. When he got to the bar, he and Velma started polishing the glasses together, their afternoon ritual.

"Ma," Don said.

"Yes, Dontchik," Velma responded, turning to get a clean rag.

"I . . . uh . . ." Don stammered.

"What is it?" Velma asked, putting down her glass.

"I want to go to my friend's house for the Fourth of July." There, he got it all out.

"What is this?" Velma asked, looking at him.

"My friend, Tomek," Don said, "is inviting me over to his house for the Fourth of July."

"But Dontchik," Velma answered, "you know we always go with Sergei to watch fireworks in Riverside Park."

"I know," Don proclaimed, "but this year I want to go to my friend's house."

"We will see about this," Velma said. "I talk to Sergei."

"Okay, Ma," Don responded.

The next day, when Don arrived at the bar, Sergei was there. Don was surprised. Sergei rarely came uptown on a weeknight.

"Don," Sergei said. "I want to talk to you."

"Okay," Don said, as he took off his jacket and hung it on the wall hook. "What do you want to talk about?"

"Your mother," Sergei said, "tells me you want to spend the Fourth of July with Tomek, is that correct?"

"Yes, at his house," Don answered.

"And where is his house?" Sergei asked.

"He lives on 84th Street, between York and East End," Don answered.

"And how long will you be there?" Sergei asked.

"Well," Don answered, "he asked me to come over around 6:00 p.m., so I guess I could be home by 9:30 p.m. or so. Is that okay?"

"I've talked with Velma about this," Sergei responded, "and I think it's time that you be able to spend holidays with your friends, if you want to."

"Really?" Don asked.

"Yes, really." Sergei responded. "You're a growing boy, and boys need to spend time with their friends as well as their families."

"Gee, Uncle Sergei," Don replied. "That's swell! Thanks!" Then Don did something he rarely did. He ran up to Sergei and he hugged him.

"Well, well," Sergei said, hugging him back, "that's okay. You have fun with your friends."

"I will, I will!" Don said.

He went around the bar to get the glasses he needed to polish, amazed at the way things had worked out. He certainly could not have predicted this.

The next day was the Fourth of July and as it was a Saturday, Don just had to go to the bar to water the plants out back, then he was free for the rest of the day. He figured he would head over to Sammy's and get his usual candy and comics, then lay around the house until it was time to go to Tomek's.

It was sweltering that day. Don got up and made himself a glass of orange juice and a bowl of cereal. Velma had already left for the bar, and Don was on his own to sit at the kitchen table and look at the comics from the day before. As he ate his cereal, and looked at the paper, Don wondered what it would be like at Tomek's tonight. He was excited, but he was also a bit nervous.

Would Tomek's parent be there? Would there be other adults on the roof? Don thought about it and realized there were very few times he was with his friends when there were no adults around. In fact, if Don really thought about it, the only times he could think of were when everyone in the neighborhood gathered on their stoops on hot summer nights.

Eventually, Don got up from the table to dress himself, so that he could go to the bar and water the plants out back. It was thick outside, humid and sticky, and Don felt no rush to get to the bar. He slowly made his way up Third, turning right at 84th, then crossed Second, until he got to the bar and saw Velma polishing the glasses through the curtained window.

"Hi, Ma," Don said, after Velma opened the Don for him.

"Hello, Dontchik," Velma said and closed the door, letting the little bells on the back make their tinkling sound that Don loved. "So hot today," she commented.

"Yeah, it is," Don said. Then he corrected himself. "I mean, yes, it is hot today." Velma hated when Don used the word *yeah*.

Don walked to the back and went out the door, finding the watering can standing against the wall. He brought it back inside and filled it from the faucet behind the bar. Then he walked back outside and proceeded to sprinkle water on the geraniums, petunias, and roses that were mostly planted in pots. They had harvested the vegetables already now that it was high summer.

When he was done, Don replaced the watering can outside the back door and said goodbye to Velma.

"I'll see you when I get home from Tomek's," Don said.

"You be good boy there, Dontchik," Velma said, giving him a pat on the head. "So big you getting."

Walking home, Don stopped off at the corner store and picked up a bottle of Coca-Cola to cool off with. Sipping it on the way, he thought about Tomek and what the celebration would be like this evening.

When he got home, he decided to distract himself with Archie and a stick of gum, while lying in bed and occasionally staring at the crack in the ceiling. As the day wore on, Don became both excited and a little nervous about going over to Tomek's.

Around 12:30, Don sat up and realized he was hungry. He put down the newspaper and made his way to the kitchen, where he opened the refrigerator and took out a roll of liverwurst, and a loaf of rye bread. He also found an onion on the counter and started to slice it thinly to add to his sandwich. Going back to open the refrigerator door, he looked for the small jar of mustard that always lived in the left-hand compartment of the refrigerator door. He got a knife out of the drawer and sliced the bread as thinly as he could, then got a match from the little tin container over the stove and opened the oven door. While he held the match above the opening on the bottom of the oven, he reached up and turned on the gas. With a whoosh, the pilot connected with the flame and Don took his sliced bread and inserted it on the top tray to be toasted.

When the bread was toasted, Don assembled his sandwich and sat down at the kitchen table, munching and reading about Archie and his antics with Jughead, Betty and Veronica. When he was done, he brought his plate to the sink, washed it, and climbed back into bed, as the circulating metal fan turned and turned on the kitchen counter.

Don didn't realize he had fallen asleep, and he felt sluggish when he woke. The air in the apartment was oppressive, and the aftertaste of the Coca-Cola had left a pasty taste in his mouth. He got out of bed and went to the kitchen to splash cold water on his face. Feeling a little better, he poured himself a glass of water, and sipped it while he looked at the clock: 5:00 p.m. Soon he could start preparing to go to Tomek's house.

While he was getting ready, he noticed the sky darkening outside. Oh, no! It isn't going to rain, is it? he wondered. He changed because his clothing was damp with sweat and by the time he finished the sun was escaping the clouds, creating a dramatic effect on the hot, sweltering streets.

Don left the apartment and made his way up Third Avenue to 84th Street, where he turned right, passing the bar, after he crossed Second Avenue. He knocked on the window to say hello to Velma, who pulled apart the curtains and waved back at Don.

When he got to Tomek's house he went up the stoop and through the front door. Pushing the round black buzzer, he waited for Tomek to come let him in. In a few minutes he heard the familiar sound of thumping footsteps on the stairs.

"Hey," Tomek said, as he opened the door for Don. "C'mon up!"

Don followed Tomek up the dimly lit staircase, which was covered in brick brown linoleum. They kept climbing.

"Geez, top floor, huh?" Don asked.

"Yup," Tomek said. "We're almost there."

When they got to the top floor, they entered the door in front of the stairs. They were in a small hallway, with the kitchen at the end and the dining room on the left. The apartment was sweltering, and no adults seemed to be home.

"Hey," Tomek said. "I got us some Coca-Colas at the store. Here's one for you. Let's head upstairs."

"Swell," said Don, accepting a cold bottle from Tomek.

"Okay, let's go," Tomek said as they headed back into the hallway and up the ladder that led to the roof. "Here's what we'll do, see? I'll put these bottles in this pack and then I'll strap it to my back. That way, we can carry the soda pop with us."

"Got it," said Don, as they placed the unopened

soda bottles in the backpack and Tomek pulled the straps over his shoulders.

When they climbed the ladder to the roof, a burst of hot air greeted them. The sun had not yet set, and Don could see mirages at the edge of the hot black roof.

Tomek pulled off the backpack and distributed the Coca-Colas. Fred and Joseph were both there, huddled over a box of firecrackers in the middle of the roof. Don peered into the box, where he saw piles of small multi-colored canisters and a long box.

"What's this?" he asked, holding up the box.

"Oh, those are Victory sparklers," Tomek said. "Those are for babies!"

"Then why do you have them?" Don asked.

"Ah, Mr. Giovanni can't get rid of 'em, so he throws 'em in every box," Tomek said.

Don held the Victory sparklers in his hands, thinking of Velma and Sergei at the picnic without him, where all the kids got their own set of sparklers to hold.

"Okay, let's go! Here," Tomek said pulling out a set of matches from his pocket.

He took a green firecracker from the box and handed it to Fred.

"Hold this," Tomek said as he struck the match, lit the tail of the firecracker, and threw it high in the sky.

The next thing Don knew, they were grabbing firecrackers from the box and lighting the fuses, then tossing them in the air as fast as possible. And then they saw other firecrackers exploding in the distance.

"Ah, here we go," Tomek complained, pointing. "They're getting started across the street. Well, we'll see about that!"

Don looked and saw where Tomek was pointing, across 84th Street, where the sky was full of brightly colored streaks of light against the smoke and the heat of the setting summer sun.

CHAPTER TWENTY-FIVE

1957

In Chicago, Don waited for a bus to take him to O'Hare International Airport. In the terminal he sat on a bench and watched all the people pass by. Taking a small notebook and lead pencil from his shirt pocket he began to sketch the scene in front of him. People were walking. There was a woman in an emerald-green dress, and a man in a navy blue suit. Behind them, there was a bright red neon sign: *Wimpy's: The Glorifed Hamburger.* Don made notes on the bottom of the page as to where the colors should go. Next time he passed an art supply store, Don decided he would buy pencils in red, green, and blue.

"Say, that's pretty good," someone said, settling down on the bench next to Don.

"Really?" Don asked, looking up at a young man who was wearing horn-rimmed glasses, a yellow checked shirt, and blue jeans.

"Sure, it is," he replied. "I like the way you've got people walking but they also look like they're standing still."

"Gee, thanks," Don said, looking back down at the sketch.

"Are you an art student?" the man asked.

"Me?" Don asked. "Well. It's funny you should ask that. Up until now, I've just fooled around. But when I return to New York, I'm going to take classes at the Art Institute."

"That's swell!" the man responded. "You're good."

"Thanks," Don said, smiling. "I really appreciate that."

"Bus number 53, bound for O'Hare International Airport, departing in ten minutes," an announcer stated on the public address system.

"Well, that's me," Don said, putting his notebook and pencil in his pocket, and picking up his backpack. "Thanks so much."

"Don't mention it," the man replied. "But do take a class," he continued. "You owe it to yourself."

"Are you a teacher?" Don asked.

"No," the man answered, "but I date a woman who studies at the Art Institute. I'm more of a writer myself."

"Wow, that's so great," Don responded. "Well, I'd better get going if I'm going to catch my bus. Thanks for the tip. It was nice talking to you."

"Anytime," the man said. "Have a good trip."

Thanks," Don said, as he began walking away. "You too!" he called over his shoulder.

As Don made his way across the terminal, he pondered the idea of a drawing class. He once took a class in school and the teacher, a woman who Don remembered as having a very deep voice, had also encouraged him. But he never did anything about it.

After boarding the bus, he settled into his seat, and took out a letter from his shirt pocket, removing it from its envelope. It was from Allison.

September 13, 1957

Dear Don,

Thank you so much for your letter. I cannot believe it! Are you really coming to Ireland? I keep pinching myself and re-reading your letter.

It would be a dream come true to see you. I am having a better time here than I expected but to have you come visit would make it all so much better!

I convinced my family that I had to continue my studies at the university. At first, they balked: "You need to help us out with Rosie," they said. "I can do both," I responded. I was going to lose my mind simply taking care of the baby, and nappies, and cooking all day long.

So, I have enrolled part-time, and take one class a week. It is just enough work to get me out of the house and have my own life and friends. I've made some good ones here, and I would love for you to meet them. They think I'm quite exotic, coming from America! I can only imagine what they'll

think of you, dark-haired, handsome boy
that you are.
  I can't wait to see you, Don.

Love,
Allison

Don blushed, as he read the last part of the letter. He closed his eyes and held it close to his chest.

What would it be like to see Allison again, and in Ireland? As Don checked in at the Aer Lingus reservation desk, he had the sense that he was not really doing this, that today was like any other day in Yorkville, that he would get up and go to school, then head over to the bar, then go home.

When he had his ticket in his hand—which he looked over several times, making sure it was real—he walked over to the waiting room, sat down, and glanced out the window. He had never been on an airplane. He had no idea what it would feel like to be on one.

Would it be like being on the wings of a bird, soaring through the sky? As he felt a tightness forming in his chest, he closed his eyes and leaned back in his seat, thinking of Allison and the time they went to see *Shane*. Alan Ladd was riding across the plains below the Grand Tetons, and Allison was passionately kissing Don. Part of him wanted to get on the plane to Ireland, and part of him wanted the familiarity of being back at the 86th Street Grande with Allison.

"Now boarding, Flight Number 104, bound for Dublin," the clerk at the reservation desk stated. Don opened his eyes. The tightness in his chest was starting to go away.

Some Notes on *Whitefish*

Whitefish came about when I was shopping for groceries.

I was in Yorkville, the old neighborhood, looking in on my eighty-eight-year-old dad and was struck by the fact that when I was growing up, there used to be three grocery stores within two blocks of my parents' apartment. When we moved to 84th Street, in 1969, there was the A&P across the street and the D'Agostino on 86th near First. Grand Union was across the street on 86th, near First. When Fairway, the closest store to my dad's apartment, almost went bankrupt in 2016, I didn't know where I would shop for him. Was I going to become part of the Fresh Direct generation?

As I walked the streets, I began to think about the stores that used to be there and all the people that had come before. There was The Gay Vienna on Second Avenue and 84th, owned by the Hungarian family of my childhood friend Vicktoria, and the Kleine Konditorei on 86th Street, where we celebrated special occasions when I was growing up. Then there was Elsie Renne's Oke Doke Bar.

Elsie was the proprietor of a dark, narrow pub at 307 East 84th Street, near Second Avenue. I passed it by for years. One evening when we were in our early twenties my boyfriend—now husband—suggested we get a drink. The bar—as well as the beers—was strictly no frills. It reminded me of the Blue and Gold, a Ukrainian bar of yesteryear on the Lower East Side. "We serve hard liquor for men who want to get drunk fast"—Sheldon Leonard's no-nonsense bartender in *It's a Wonderful Life* could have uttered these lines in either of these establishments.

There was, however, something more to these bars: there was ethnic community. Yorkville still had German and Hungarian residents when I was little. There were many Jewish people from all over. My family was from Russia and Ukraine.

As I passed the old bar, which is now an Italian restaurant at the time of this writing, I thought about the way the neighborhood looked and felt during another era and I got an idea about a boy raised tending bar for his mother. What would that childhood look like? How would he be the same or different from the other kids in the neighborhood? And what would the relationship be between the bar and its patrons?

Around this time, on my block in Brooklyn, I was lending money to a neighbor who was always a little down and out. Marie asked for a loan on a regular basis, but she also returned the money and often asked me to hold a little extra for her. "You're the Susu?" my friend Danielle, asked. "What's a Susu?" I wanted to know.

Whitefish is part immigrant story, part Bildungsroman, with a little Rumspringa thrown in at the end, but it is also about money and the way in which ethnic communities support each other when they are still new to the New World.

Few people now know the Yorkville that once was. I am so grateful I got a sense of its final moments when I was growing up. I hoped to bring back the sounds, sights, and smells of the old neighborhood. Mostly, I needed to get a sense of its people.

Ultimately, it was a joy to imagine, research and recreate a world that was once a vibrant ethnic enclave in midcentury Manhattan.

Acknowledgments

It is extraordinary that the research on Yorkville—a former immigrant enclave in what is now known as the Upper East Side in Manhattan—was mostly found at my fingertips as I wrote on my home computer. Previously, this work would have been done at the library.

Because I grew up watching TV and old movies with my parents, visual images were often as powerful for me as written words. The photographs I found confirmed something I had grown aware of as I walked the streets of Yorkville; when the weather was warm, ethnic communities once made the sidewalks and stoops their back yards. They sat, gossiped, drank, and watched their kids play stickball, roller skate, and run screaming through ice-cold fire hydrant sprays. Today people stay indoors, partially because of air conditioning—to say nothing of a world of electronic distractions—but also because we communicate less face to face.

I am grateful that former residents of Yorkville

posted online comments that accompanied the photographs I found. They formed an oral history of sorts and helped me envision a world I had only known the periphery of. In addition, the writing of Kathryn Jolowicz, President of the Yorkville/Kleindeutschland Historical Society, brought this vibrant neighborhood to life.

The members of the Writer's Circle at the New York Public Library Mulberry Street branch were invaluable in their support, reading early chapters and helping me with research. Librarian Sherri Machlin made it all happen and to her I owe a massive debt. Alexa Recio de Fitch kindly offered to be my first reader. I cannot thank her enough. In addition, my late uncle, Reuben, and my good friend, Randolf Treu, served as readers whose input was invaluable. Christine Summerson took on the admirable task of being a repeat, in-depth reader, providing me with guidance, detailed notes, and a pile of questions that helped me understand where I needed to go with the next draft. I'm thrilled my good friend, Kate Hornstein, moved back to New York and ended up in Yorkville; she gave me marvelous suggestions and introduced me to the Webster Branch of the New York Public Library, an immigrant haven back in the day. Ultimately, it was Christine and Kate who challenged me to turn *Whitefish* into a novel, moving it away from the comfortable novella format where it originally started. "I wanted more," Kate said. This is a comment I've heard about my writing numerous times, and I take it as the highest compliment and ultimate challenge.

The reference librarians at the 42nd street branch of the New York Public Library were extremely helpful in providing historical information on Yorkville.

Danielle Simon enlightened me about the *susu,* an informal bank that is started by members of an immigrant community in the New World. Danielle and I, sitting on my stoop in Brooklyn, often wondered at the many similarities between immigrant cultures, whether they are from Africa, the Caribbean or Eastern Europe. "Wait—your family did that, too?!" we would howl to each other.

Another volume could be written about the role of food in immigrant culture and I was lucky enough to be a part of my friend Vicktoria's world at The Gay Vienna, a Hungarian restaurant owned by her parents, Nandor and Elizabeth Veress, in the early 1970s. My dear friend, writer Les Bohem, also the son of a Hungarian immigrant, served as final reader, and enough cannot be said about his enthusiasm for this project.

Writers who independently publish are faced with the challenge of finding their own designers. For decades I have been blessed with the friendship and extraordinary vision of Jonathan D. Lippincott, who has lovingly designed my books and to whom I owe a debt of gratitude.

And I just happen to be the mother of Niko Prytula, who has collaborated with me on several of my projects culminating in the cover art of the book you hold in your hands.

If I didn't have the constant encouragement of my marvelous friends and family this book would not have been written. A first novel is quiet, solitary work and the focus entailed often means you're grabbing your phone or opening your laptop to "get something down." I'm grateful my family understood and gave me the space to make it happen.

Finally, I owe a debt of gratitude to my late father and mother, who relocated our family to Yorkville when I was four. If my mother hadn't moved us to a neighborhood that was closer to her new job at the United Nations, I would never have experienced the special place that Yorkville was in the 1960s and '70s.

About the Author

Anita Bushell is the author of *Object Essays: A Collection* (2022), and the editor of *Writing In a Library: Poems by Maria Prytula* (2017) and *Lilacs in the Spring: Meditations on the Life of Maria Prytula* (2016). She has written for *The Artisanal Writer*, *Bristol Noir*, the *San Antonio Review*, *Friends Journal*, *Grande Dame Literary*, *Apple in the Dark*, *Motherwell*, the *Linewaiters' Gazette*, and *Uncensored: American Family Experiences with Poverty and Homelessness*.

anitabushell.com